some
of
the
parts

Colleen O. Potocki

Blue Heeler Books LLC

Chapbook Press

Schuler Books

2660 28th Street SE

Grand Rapids, MI 49512

(616) 942-7330

www.schulerbooks.com

Some of the Parts

ISBN 13: 9781966196341

eBook ISBN: 9781966196358

Library of Congress Control Number: 2025918309

Printed in the United States by Chapbook Press.

Some of the Parts is an autobiography, a collection of words, thoughts, and stories from my life, birth to adulthood. The stories are told as I remember them and have written them. Some names have been changed and details omitted to respect privacy. The dialogue is drafted and developed from memory. Events are arranged mostly in chronological order but sometimes placed where they make structural sense.
All that said, this is my life as lived. Parts of it.

to Jennifer, Jane, and Chris

1

I was born on September 11, 1963. 9-11-1963. I have a birthright affection for odd numbers. No belief in superstitions or omens. Just an odd leaning.

Mom believed in luck and signs. She told me her "Two Crows" story more than once:

"Farris and I were driving in Ontario and stopped at McDonald's for coffee and various food items for the road. With a vaguely distressed look on her face, the cashier said, 'Would you like to add an item to change your total?' I asked her why and she pointed to the total on the cash register: $6.66.

I stared at her a second and then, like a flash of lightning, a thought came to my brain. 'It's okay,' I said. 'As we were just driving in, I saw two crows a' flying.' With a look of relief, the cashier nodded her head and let me pay.

I silently gave thanks to my Irish childhood and memory of the rhyme:

'One crow, sorrow.
Two crows, joy.
Three crows, a girl.
Four crows, a boy.
Five crows, silver.
Six crows, gold.
Seven crows, a secret never to be told.'

The joy of two crows flying canceled out the dark side of $6.66."

It was hard to not look at Mom with a sideways glance sometimes.

2

I had no input in my naming other than my early arrival.

My mom was born Mary Kathleen. My dad, Farris Moore. Both Canadians. That said, Dad was born on a kitchen table in Maine. An anchor baby. Birthright citizenship. He served in the United States Marine Corps. After his service, Dad married Mom and moved to the United States.

I was born in Indiana at St. Joseph's Hospital. Two months early, weighing just over three pounds. The odds of my survival were lower than low. Mom was unconscious, so the nurses named me Ann. I was baptized, confirmed, and christened without delay. Death expected.

The attending doctor insisted I was not going to make it. Sixteen days later, I was still alive. Mom decided to name me something other than Ann. She did not go with the name she had planned to use: Kathleen. Her middle name. As Mom told it, "We did not want to make a painful situation more painful. Colleen was chosen because it means 'girl' in Irish."

As Dad told it, "Colleen has a detached, almost clinical meaning. Practical, in case of death." I spent two months in an incubator infrequently touched by human hands. Eventually, I was strong enough to leave St. Joseph's Hospital.

I was sent home to meet my siblings. Mom had three babies in a span of 27 months. All daughters. Jennifer, Jane, Colleen. My parents referred to us as Irish triplets. Irish triplets was a celebratory expression in our household. Used with a hint of hubris. My brother Chris would come three years later.

My sister Jennifer says my coming home from the hospital is her earliest memory, claiming I looked like an angel. I am guessing Jennifer overheard my parents talking about the likelihood I would die.

3

Both Mom and I had near-death experiences during childhood. I was dangerously premature; my mom had a bout of illness. Mom called it her "Cold Room" story:

"During our visits to Fredericton, New Brunswick, Farris and I usually stayed at the Ramada Inn. It has a large, comfortable lounge in the swimming pool area. Our various family members would come by to visit in the evenings. One such evening my sister Dorothy, her husband John, Farris, and I were sitting around a table reminiscing about our early days.

Dorothy and I were remembering how cold the winters were and how our family and many others coped with the freezing temperatures by moving our summer kitchen into the living room – stove, table, chairs – everything moved into the living room-leaving the kitchen bare except for kindling wood to start the fire – we called it the Cold Room.

Dorothy almost casually said, 'You know the story of how you almost ended up in the Cold Room, don't you?' I said I didn't know what she was talking about.

She proceeded to tell me about the winter when I was the baby of the family of seven – sister Dorothy and five brothers – Basil was not yet born. Everyone in the family was extremely sick except my mother – probably with scarlet fever according to oldest brother Greg. As the story goes, I was the sickest of all.

When Dr. McGrand from Fredericton Junction dropped around to check on us, he told my mother and father that even if I survived, I would undoubtedly be deaf, blind, and possibly dumb. He said, 'Just put her in the Cold Room and she will just slip away in her sleep.'

My mother and father were aghast that he would even suggest such a thing. My father was furious. My mother spent the next days and weeks ministering to us all. I do remember her telling me once that when I was very small, she spent days and nights draining the passages of my ears, nose, and throat endlessly.

Anyhow, a few weeks later Dr. McGrand came back to check on the family. He was sitting in the living room and asked my father, 'Where's the dead baby?'

At that moment I came toddling into the room. My father said, 'There's your dead baby!' Dr. McGrand appeared stunned, and after a long moment, said, 'All I can say is your wife must be some nurse.'

Farris was doing extensive genealogy at the time on our New Brunswick families. We noticed that more often than not there were one, two, sometimes three or four early childhood deaths in our farm families. Some were buried in cemeteries and others were buried by a chosen tree on the farm.

I had the thought after Dorothy's revelation that perhaps some of those little ones went to sleep in the Cold Room."

4

I weighed just over 3 pounds at birth. If I were an angel, I would be a small angel. But only for a short period.

I inherited Dad's size 10 bones, maybe nearer size 12 bones. Jennifer and Jane, my two sisters, have Mom's size 6 bones, maybe nearer size 4 bones. I was the youngest daughter and the biggest daughter, yet Mom still approached dressing me from a top-down perspective, passing Jennifer's and Jane's clothes my way after they outgrew them.

Mom was blind to the reality before her: age and body size are not co-dependent variables. The older sibling is not always the bigger sibling. Mom did not always have the time to consider the minutia of parenting, so I spent the first thirteen years wedging myself into small clothes. Dad perhaps could have noticed my dilemma; however, I was raised during a time when mothers took care of the clothing. And Mom was too busy to do so. Understandable.

Mom and Dad were business owners—long work weekdays and weekends. No worries. I dealt with my farm stock build. And I dealt with the doll-like stature of my sisters. Acceptance. Not complete acceptance, but only occasional bouts of inadequacy fed by female celebrities. Movie stars and supermodels, from Twiggy to Brooke Shields.

I admired my mom. Mom was beautiful, busy, and smart, but mostly busy. She was a working mom when working moms were uncommon. She was not the only working mother in our neighborhood; however, the two other working mothers were a nurse and a teacher. Their schedules, I hope, were slightly kinder, allowing a consideration of home-cooked meals, housecleaning, and child size.

Jennifer and Jane also have Mom's dark brown, nearly black hair. Chris and I have Dad's dirty dishwater brown hair. Genetics. Genetics aside, Mom and Dad held the responsibility for the naming of their four children: Jennifer, Jane, Colleen, and Chris. Solid names. Plain names. No wildcard awful name or exotic name.

The letter pattern though invites subsets: J, J, C, C. Two J names followed by two C names created a divide that sometimes felt like a chasm between my sisters and me. I was no longer part of the Irish triplets the instant Chris was named. Jennifer and Jane. Colleen and Chris. A new paradigm.

In later years, Jennifer and Jane went to an elite private school; Chris and I went to public school. I did get to go to the local parochial for one year of high school. Dad and Mom had a set amount of time and resources, seemingly allocated according to birth order. The law of diminishing returns for Chris and me.

There was equality: All four of us walked away from childhood with our parents' work ethic.

5

Dad and Mom worked from early morning to evening, Monday – Friday and on Saturday. Jennifer, Jane, Chris, and I did our clueless best to live each day. We raised ourselves while our parents were building a business and gaining financial security. Dad and Mom provided the four of us with a behavioral electric fence of sorts: Catholicism. The threat of eternal damnation coupled with the possibility of Dad's anger weighed upon our individual and collective decision-making.

Jennifer was a good de facto guardian. She walked me to school and back home each weekday. I walked two steps behind Jennifer and Jane. The sidewalk wasn't quite wide enough for the three of us. Plus, Jennifer and Jane liked to talk to each other. I was extremely shy. Talking was painful. My head was the only place that felt safe. I spent a good deal of time in my head. Often described on report cards as "a rich inner life." A euphemism.

At school, I thought my thoughts and did my best to meet expectations without calling attention to myself. I had coping strategies. My black, grey, white plaid dress had a scarlet rick rack trim along the bottom hem; I ran my finger along the trim to stay calm. And my light green dress had three buttons sewn in a vertical row just beneath the Peter Pan collar. One yellow. One blue. One red. I touched those buttons often.

I followed directions. Completed lessons without struggle. Excelled at parallel play. Flunked associative play—not ready for direct interaction with classmates. When pushed to engage, tears fell. Teachers graciously let me orbit the social aspects of class. Most of the time. I slowly learned to answer questions aloud and to play with others at recess. Slowly.

In second grade, I built up enough courage to join the reading circle, legs dutifully crisscrossed. I loved books. All was good—until the day no clean underwear was in the underwear drawer. Empty. Not a crisis. I slipped on shorts.

That afternoon, when I crisscrossed for reading circle, the teacher gasped. I noticed her notice. I looked where she was looking. Then I noticed what she noticed. I immediately uncrossed and teared up. My teacher gave me a kind smile and nodded for me to sit at my desk. I removed myself from the circle.

6

We lived in a cookie-cutter house. Southeast Michigan. My parents' first home purchase. A $19,000 three-bedroom, one bathroom ranch home. A single luxury feature: a laundry chute. The laundry chute was located in the main floor bathroom. A small metal door, painted white, concealed the chute. The chute was a rectangular hole situated directly above the laundry section of the basement where the washer and dryer sat.

Two design flaws. #1: Location. The chute door was about 12 inches in front of the toilet seat. It is indelicate to talk about toilets, but the proximity of the clothes chute in relation to the toilet invited misuse. #2: Spring-loaded hinges. If a child were to open the chute door and let go of the door handle, it whapped shut. A loud metallic whap. When Chris or I used the bathroom, a whap, whap, whap could be heard throughout the house. Until Dad yelled, "Cut it out!" Jennifer and Jane never messed with the chute. No interest. I am not going to dissect their disinterest.

For me, a visit to the bathroom was coupled with a secondary urge: an irrepressible want to throw something down the chute. A bar of soap. Chris's toothbrush. A Barbie Doll. A bottle of Dad's Vitalis Hair Tonic. Occasionally, there was a chute jam—which was a minor or major family event, depending on Dad's mood.

Dad was a no-frills dad. For him, the laundry chute was a test of character. He was not used to luxury. The laundry chute worried him. Too fancy. A slippery slope to raising weak, soft children. Mostly, the laundry chute was just a laundry chute. It served its utilitarian purpose: creating a mountain of clothes in the basement. Untended. Out of sight. Out of mind.

Our basement took in more than laundry. Holiday decorations, suitcases, leftover kitchen tiles, cans of paint, boxes of books that would never lose their funky damp smell, and more. The basement was also home to a little white mouse. Snowflake. Snowflake escaped from her pet cage. We had a sibling meeting and decided it was best not to share the news of Snowflake's escape with our parents.

A few weeks later, as my mom reached into the laundry pile to begin sorting clothes, Snowflake was found. Alive. Luckily, Dad was not in the house to hear Mom's scream. After getting over her fright, Mom told us to leave food and water out for Snowflake. She also told us that it was okay if Dad did not know about Snowflake's escape. He had enough to worry about.

When Jennifer began junior high school, Dad built her a basement bedroom. I was jealous for about one second. The basement was one whisper away from the Cold Room—dark, drafty, cluttered. Home to a rodent.

7

Dad was larger than life—hardworking and intimidating. When he was home, Chris and I would follow him around in hopes he would decide to play with us. Dad needed downtime from work, so we mostly watched him read magazines or eat snacks.

Dad had a penchant for red pistachio nuts. The household budget was tight. Pistachios were an extravagant purchase. A rare indulgence. When Dad settled on our brown couch ready to enjoy a single-serving bag of red pistachios, Chris and I sat on the floor near his feet, ready for any cast-offs from the Nut King. Chris and I could make a game out of any situation. If Dad happened to find a pistachio that was completely closed or impossible to open, he would pass it our way. Chris and I took turns cracking each rejected shell with our teeth to get to the salty nut inside. Doing so, stained our fingers red. It felt feral.

When Dad did play with Chris and me, there was an edge of fear. Mostly a good fear, though still scary. Dad made up this game to play with us called Blanket Monster. A night game. He would turn off all the lights in the house. Except the nightlight in the bathroom. Tell us to hide. He then put a blanket over his head, and a howling blanket monster would try to find us. Chris and I loved it, but I wet my pants once or twice. Fright-induced incontinence.

8

Jennifer, Jane, Chris, and I went to Catechism after school on Wednesdays. Jennifer's Catechism teacher once announced, "Jennifer is the only student in this room going to Heaven." Jennifer had done her homework. Our whole family went to church on Sunday. Stories and singing.

On Sunday, I would hunker down in the pew and read the parables in the missal. Parable. Missal. Comforting words. I read and reread the stories. Spiritual. Didactic. Meaningful—not the Parable of the Prodigal Son though. The story is actually about two sons, not one. One son does what he is supposed to do. Meets his family responsibilities. The other son does not. He leaves home, wastes money—and a host of other transgressions. A wayward son. Expansively so. There is even a mention of prostitutes. When the prodigal son comes home, his father embraces him, celebrates him, forgives him. A fatted calf is killed for his welcome home meal. The son in the parable who dutifully stayed home. Consistently and quietly good. No embrace. No celebration. No fatted calf. Maybe I would understand when I was older.

At church, Jennifer sat on one side of me. Dad sat on the other. When we were cued to sing a hymn, Jennifer and I belted out the songs, listening to see who messed up first. There was happiness in this game. Dad was not a church dad. He attended. He wanted to be elsewhere. If I ever forgot myself and rested my hand on the pew in front of me, Dad placed his hand on top of my hand and pressed down. Crushing my hand. Challenging me to wince. It was a game. I liked it.

I have few memories of Mom and Dad ever touching me. We were not a touchy family. No hugs, handholding, or lap sitting. Occasional spankings, yes. Church hand crushing, yes.

9

When I was 8 years old, Mom enrolled me in piano lessons. The catch: We didn't own a piano. I had to practice on a paper keyboard. Once a week I attended a piano class where I played the assigned song for my teacher on an actual piano—hearing the music for the first time. I was in a class of 10 girls. Our weekly lesson involved each girl taking a turn playing the song-of-the-week on the classroom piano. As each budding pianist played, the instructor gave a loud, very public critique. He was brutal. At the end of class, he assigned the next week's melody. I kept at my lessons. After all, it was quite magical to hear a song after a week of soundless practicing.

The best song was titled "Little Ostrich Chicks." It was the first song I played on our new household piano which was eventually secured by my parents. I didn't realize it at the time, but "Little Ostrich Chicks" had the same tune as "Whistle While You Work," the classic *Snow White* tune. I still remember every word:

"Little ostrich chicks
Quickly will grow up
They'll grow up, be 6 feet tall
And weigh 300 pounds
Even though they're birds
Ostriches can't fly
Nonetheless, I must confess
They do run very fast"

Soon after getting the piano, I quit playing. I found practice more grueling with an actual piano in the house. Public. Loud. Plus, I discovered Nancy Drew books. *The Secret of the Old Clock* and many more.

Mom decided to learn to play the piano. Someone had to play the piano. We owned it. I only ever heard her practicing one song: "Both Sides Now," by Joni Mitchell. Over and over. I quietly sang along wherever I happened to be in the house.

10

Dad tried to teach me how to swim in a Holiday Inn pool. His method: Sink or swim. He simply threw me into the deep end of the hotel pool.

I did not know how to swim. I struggled, then sank in the green water. Dad eventually saved me. Let me rest for a few minutes. Then he threw me in again. I struggled in the water. Sank, a second time. Dad saved me. I rested in wary fear. Dad was stubborn. He threw me in the pool a third time. I didn't struggle. What was the point? I contentedly sank. Dad saved me. I sensed his disappointment.

Dissatisfied that when put in a sink or swim situation I did not choose to swim.

11

In second grade, my class had a robot contest. The robot contest came at the end of a long school day. I cannot remember the exact context. I remember the rules though: students were to move like robots on the carpeted area of the classroom. When the teacher shouted "Freeze," all robots had to stop moving. Power down. The student-robot who could stay perfectly still while in powered down mode won the contest.

At the start of the game, there were many student-robots on that carpet. Then, the teacher called, "Freeze!" A few students were immediately out of the game—unable to freeze themselves for even a few seconds. The usual suspects. The rest of us tried not to breathe. One-by-one, any student who moved—even slightly—was called out. Booted off the carpet. Figuratively. Even blinking was cause for dismissal. I ended up one of the last two students left on the carpet. One of the last two powered down robots. Then, I blinked. But no one saw me. A mere two seconds later, the other remaining student was called out for some miniscule movement. I was quickly pinned with the prize: a heavyweight construction paper circle decorated with two long pieces of stiff, velvety ribbon. A teacher-made badge of honor. In the middle of the white circle were the words, "Best Robot." I won before I could even consider if I had cheated.

Questions remained. If a powered down robot is indeed powered down, would the powered down robot know if he or she blinked? No. So by not confessing I was just staying in character. Right? Further. If a powered down robot blinks but no one sees it, did the powered down robot officially, explicitly move? Arguably no. My "Best Robot" experience left me confused. Did I win? I could rationalize my way to a win. But then, does the need to rationalize, by default, mean I really lost? A moot point. In second grade, I was too shy to speak up. I let the teacher celebrate my robot skills. I stayed quiet.

I do not have a photograph of my "Best Robot" moment, but somewhere, in a box in the garage, I have two school pictures—kindergarten and fourth grade—a few essays written in high school, and my "Best Robot" ribbon. I kept it over the years. Not sure why. The contest felt like a defining moment.

12

When I was in 4th grade, my teacher Mrs. Potter left the classroom for some type of urgent need. Before she left the class alone, she firmly ordered, "Stay in your seats. Do not leave your chairs." Well, as soon as the teacher was out-of-sight, Brad left his chair. He grabbed my painting of a plesiosaurus off the drying rack and ran around the classroom with it. My plesiosaurus painting was created to accompany my plesiosaurus report.

I had no talent as an artist; however, I transcended my ability-level with my plesiosaurus painting. Not luck. Mathematical reality. A take on the infinite monkey theorem. A monkey hitting random typewriter keys for an infinite amount of time will eventually type every existing finite text—Shakespeare even. So, it stands to reason, a student, even an artistically challenged student, given enough art assignments, will create at least one masterpiece.

The plesiosaurus was my masterpiece and Brad had it. I jumped out of my seat and chased Brad around the room. I snatched my painting from his hands. While I inspected it for damage, Brad slid into his chair. Seconds later, Mrs. Potter came back from the office. I was caught standing. Mrs. Potter did not ask questions. She commanded that I come to the front of the classroom. On my way to meet my consequence, I carefully returned my beloved plesiosaurus to the drying rack.

Mrs. Potter made an example of my disobedience. She took down the big red paddle that hung on the big hook on the wall. I was paddled in front of the class. Three whacks. Each whack reminded me of the laundry chute. The public humiliation should have birthed any suppressed artistic talent I had. That did not happen. I did, however, paint a fairly nifty Gila monster a few years later to accompany my report on Gila monsters.

13

Mom purchased individual-size boxes of Cracker Jacks caramel popcorn for my sisters and me to enjoy as we watched our one evening of television per week: *Brady Bunch*, *Nanny and the Professor*, or *The Partridge Family*.

Our brother Chris was still too young to eat popcorn. I have a hazy memory of Aunt Shirley, a nurse, lecturing my mom on the evils of eating popcorn before age 5.

Each box of Cracker Jacks came with a prize inside. Jennifer, Jane, and I looked forward to opening the prize envelope, but there was apprehension. The prize could be a miniature thrill: a pinball game, a necklace charm, or a whistle. The prize could also be a miniature disappointment: a plastic replica of a hot dog or a green army man. Not okay. Jennifer once had a curious surprise in her Cracker Jack box: a perfectly sealed prize envelope with no prize inside.

Jennifer did not open it. She instead wrote a letter to the Cracker Jack company and enclosed the defective prize envelope. A few weeks later, Jennifer received a box in the mail from Cracker Jacks, containing about twenty prizes. With an official letter thanking Jennifer for bringing the problem to their attention.

I was jealous of the prizes, but more of Jennifer's ability to communicate with a big corporation.

14

Out of necessity, I defined a friend as someone who lived in my neighborhood who would eat school lunch with me every day. My childhood friend Tilda and I could not have been more different. Tilda was bold, daring, and brash. I was shy, quiet, and obedient. Tilda had a habit that I endured. Every lunch period, Tilda would dump out my brown bag lunch and evaluate the contents. My lunch was the same nearly every day: a sandwich, an apple or orange or pear, and a bag of chips. Rarely any variation. I disliked pears. Tilda inventoried my lunch bag contents, expressed dissatisfaction, and then let me get on with my meal.

Once in a blue moon, however, my mom stopped at the local bakery and purchased a big shortbread smiley-faced cookie, painted with yellow icing, chocolate eyes and smile. No nose. The thoughtful consideration of Mom and the surprise element brought me happiness. Once in about every 50 lunches or so, my lunch bag contained a smiley-faced cookie. On these days, Tilda would dump out my lunch, squeal with delight, and then break the smiley-faced cookie in half. One piece for her. One piece for me.

I was arguably the victim of a crime. I did not see it that way. I internally rationalized that if I knew I was being taken advantage of and I allowed it, then I was not a victim. I was the one in control. My adult friend Marlene would disagree. Marlene is wonderful and never steals cookies from me. Her personal mantra though is blunt: Control is an illusion.

15

My earliest memory of standardized test-taking is not a good one.
Fifth grade. The Iowa Test of Basic Skills. The ITBS.

A nervous girl threw up during the administration of the test. The gooey,
brown pellets in the girl's vomitus drew immediate attention. As if part
of the standardized test, students raced to identify the mysterious
dark blobs.

A. "Ewww. Her teeth were pushed out with the puke."
B. "No way, those are rabbit droppings."
C. "Gross—maybe they are pieces of her stomach."
D. None of the above.

Teachers were unsettled. The testing environment had been
compromised. Students were asked to close their test booklets, to tuck
the scantron sheet neatly inside, and to put down their No. 2 pencils.
Students were then dismissed to recess while Mrs. Harris called the ITBS
hotline to get instructions on how to proceed.

I should not have had Raisin Bran for breakfast when in the throes of
standardized testing.

16

My sisters and I had very few toys. The lean years. During the long days
of summer, we made up games to pass the time.

One game was called "Sears Catalog." The game had one playing piece:
a thick catalog from Sears—a household staple back in the day. Heavy,
inches thick, filled with pictures of clothing, furniture, tools, and toys.
The game involved a time-limit, budget, and shopping mission. The

objective: who could make the best use of her money by completing the shopping mission within the prescribed time limit. Once, for example, we set a budget of $3,000 to refurbish our three-bedroom, one-bath house.

One-by-one, my sisters and I were allowed 30 minutes each with the catalog to make a list of intended purchases, write down page numbers, and record prices. After our catalog time, we each gave an elaborate presentation of a proposed purchase plan. In an unanticipated move, my sister Jane furnished the household bedrooms with mattresses only, no headboards or frames. She argued it was a bohemian design style. I was awed by her use of the word bohemian and knew I had lost as soon as she uttered the word. Jennifer and I were traditional and practical. Jane had imagination, no boundaries.

We also had a Burpee plant catalog in the house. Jennifer and Jane wanted nothing to do with Burpee. I would spend hours planning and drawing gardens for a range of budgets. The pictures of flowers and exotic names were mesmerizing. No matter my price range, I determined, "No marigolds." Dad was marigold crazy and had planted them in huge bunches around our back patio. Monochromatic orange blooms everywhere. His landscaping quest was driven by a single love: low maintenance.

When Dad realized my interest in gardening, he approved. He didn't give me any money, but he gave me a small plot of land on one side of the house. A stretch about 6 feet long and 3 feet wide. It was all mine. I mapped out my flower garden and used my allowance savings to buy seeds, bulbs, and seedlings—dahlias, carnations, nasturtiums, sunflowers, zinnia, snapdragons, and some anemones. Six strawberry plants. And one rose plant. It was agonizing trying to decide which rose plant to purchase. In a rare moment of agrarian interest, Mom suggested the Peace Rose. A yellow bloom imbued with a hue of pink. I quickly agreed. My purchase arrived. I planted, watered, and waited. Every plant thrived, except for the anemones. After two-months, I dug up the anemone seeds and mailed them back to Burpee. I did not get a refund; instead, Burpee mailed me a couple of seed packets as restitution: marigold seeds. Heavy disappointment. The Peace Rose bloomed and bloomed.

As my summer of planting closed, Tilda and I were hanging out by the flower garden. My mom disapproved of Tilda. Often. In our boredom, Tilda dared me to see how many rose petals I could shove up my nose. Before accepting the challenge, I astutely asked, "One nostril or two?" One. I plucked off a slightly wilting Peace Rose bloom. Petal by petal, I shoved the flower up my nose. I don't remember how many petals I fit in. Tilda and I giggled ourselves to tears. Removing the petals ended up harder than putting them in. As Mom and I drove to the emergency clinic, she told me I was never to play with Tilda again and warned me that I might have lasting brain damage if the doctors were unable to get all the petals out of my nose.

The rose petal incident, an unthinking moment. My most memorable childhood misstep—action before thought, excitabilities over inhibitors, peer acceptance over family approval. I choose to think of it as bohemian.

17

My mom fed me crossword puzzles and seek-and-find books. She liked to keep my mind busy. I tended to overthink. My overthinking led to overimagining which led to overfearing everything.

When I learned about infinity, my worldview was shattered. I always assumed that 1-2-3-4 was leading somewhere. The existence of infinity, however, meant that as I counted forward, I was not in fact getting closer to an end. If I am moving forward but forward has no end, am I still moving forward? The futility of counting panicked me.

As a child, I loved words. I knew many words but not how to pronounce them. When I read, I saw the words in my mind without a soundtrack. The words were seen and understood. Not heard. Known, not uttered. Mispronunciation became a paralyzing fear.

My sister Jane was tasked with accompanying me to any birthday
party I was invited to because I was too scared to go by myself.
Too many unknowns.

In advanced math, I cried because I was required to solve problems on
the chalkboard in front of the class. I begged to be moved to grade-level
math where problems were solved quietly and privately at one's desk.
My wish was granted. Not sure if that was one step forward or two
steps back.

18

We had an A-frame swing set in our backyard. An inexpensive metal
swing set. Two swings, a glider, and a slide. Dad, who was usually
cement crazy, did not cement the four legs of the swing set into the
ground. It was still reasonably safe, although not fully anchored. When a
swinger swung to a certain height, the back legs of the swing set would
rise up and then down, making a thump every time the poles returned to
their respective holes in the ground. The rhythmic thump was satisfying,
like the laundry chute. I spent time on that swing set. Much time.

Eventually. The glider broke. Then, the swings. The slide bent to one-
side—still usable though. For a while, Dad let the chains of the swings
hang without their broken seats. Four hanging chains. Chris and I
invented chain games. Adventures to act out. Most of our games included
swinging the chains at each other as hard as we could. Not in a mean
way. We were playing. After the eye injury incident, Dad took down
the chains.

No matter. The swing set still had use. The lopsided slide and the
frame remained. New game. Chris and I climbed up the slide and then
shimmied across the top bar of the swing set on our bottoms. We'd scoot
to the middle, drop upside down, release our hands, and hang using our
knees as hooks. A simple game. Whoever could hang the longest was the

winner. We had to be careful. A fall might involve broken bones. The height factor, while thrilling, was reckless.

One day when Chris was not around, I decided to practice hanging. I climbed up the slide and scooted myself to the middle of the top bar. I took a deep breath for bravery—flipped upside down and let go. I was determined to hang for as long as possible. Nature had other plans.

As I was hanging, a swarm of wasps circled my head. I tried to carefully shoo them away without falling. This angered the wasps. I was bitten multiple times on my face and arms. I was scared to scream because a wasp might fly in my mouth. I quietly struggled and fell to the ground. I was surprised I did not die. Sore and bruised, I fled to the shade of the backyard apple tree and hugged my knees to my chest. I sat there for hours. Until I heard my parents' car pulling into the driveway. Home from work.

I ran to Mom and told her I was stung. We visited the bathroom medicine chest. She put a drop of Mercurochrome on each swollen bite. I felt better. I was done with the swing set.

19

Most of our extended family lived in a faraway land: New Brunswick, Canada. We traveled there about once a year. One visit, I was dropped at my grandmother's farm to stay for a week. It was wonderful. Animals everywhere. On the large wooden farmhouse porch, two massive Newfoundland dogs panted. Anywhere I decided to go, they followed. Most often, I headed for the cows.

Every morning, my grandmother's cows would depart into the woods to escape the heat and flies. I liked their gradual exodus from the yard and watched until the last cow disappeared into the trees. Around dinner time, I positioned myself on the wooden fence and waited for the cows' return. A first cow eventually sauntered back home. I stayed until the yard was packed with cows. By the end of the week, I earned the trust of the cows. I picked handfuls of grass; they would eat it from my flat hand.

After we returned home, I begged my parents for a dog. My dad believed animals belonged on farms, not in a three-bedroom, one-bath house that already sheltered six humans.

The one pet moment Dad and I shared was watching *Old Yeller* together. At his suggestion. I cried. I was convinced Dad had me watch the film to quell my near constant campaign for a dog. His unspoken lecture: "See, Colleen, if we get a dog, it will tussle with a rabid wolf, and I will have to put it down." I remained dog-obsessed.

For my birthday, my parents bought me *The AKC American Kennel Club Book*—containing glossy photos and descriptions of all registered dog breeds—over 220 breeds. I read it. And reread it, mesmerized by the Rhodesian Ridgeback, the Komondor, the Afghan Hound.

20

I sometimes convinced Chris to play Dogs with me. The premise was simple: We each chose a dog breed and dog name; then, pretended to be dogs. I always picked Collie. Chris and I crawled around the house on our knees, panted, barked, growled. We licked water out of cereal bowls placed on the floor. Cereal became dog food, and we gobbled it off dinner plates with our dog tongues. We rubbed our dog heads against Jennifer's and Jane's legs, whimpering for them to pet us or scratch our dog bellies. They screamed and ran away. Part of the fun.

21

Dad and Mom took us to a drive-in double feature: *Willy Wonka and the Chocolate Factory* with Gene Wilder followed by *The Way We Were* starring Barbra Streisand and Robert Redford.

Willy Wonka and the Chocolate Factory had a liberating impact: Varuca Salt. A character written to be unliked. Varuca was a spoiled child. I knew it was probably wrong to love Varuca, but I could not help it. Varuca was unabashedly spoiled. She yelled, "Where's my Golden Ticket! I want my Golden Ticket!" She demanded, "I want an Oompa-Loompa!" And she insisted, "I want a Golden Goose now, Daddy!" Seeing Varuca throw a fit was shocking and thrilling. I was delighted by Varuca's bold behavior. She said what she wanted to say. And I did not have to worry about Varuca's soul. Varuca was a fictional being.

My parents put pillows and blankets in our station wagon, because we were expected to fall asleep after *Willy Wonka*. I didn't fall asleep. I watched *The Way We Were*. The movie confused me. Why did smart Katie put up with ne'er-do-well Hubbell? And one movie line twisted my young brain: "Are you really so sure about everything you're so sure about?"

At the time, I wasn't sure about much. I didn't need an adult movie messing with my head. It did.

22

My parents piled my siblings and me into the station wagon to go to London, Ontario to visit my mom's brother and family. Not so far as New Brunswick.

Chris and I were relegated to the third row in the station wagon. Our station wagon had a rear-facing third seat. I believe it was a Ford Country Squire, complete with faux wood panels. As a profoundly shy child, I found the rear-facing seat awkward. I was subjected to long, self-conscious moments staring at the car driver situated immediately behind us. I never knew what was appropriate. Should I smile? Should I wave? Should I pretend to look at scenery to the right and left of me? Should I simply keep looking forward at the driver pretending that we don't see each other. My brother Chris had a ready go-to strategy: he put his blanket over his head, avoiding all discomfort, leaving me alone in blanketless duress.

Road trips to visit our London cousins were less than ideal. Mom's side of the family has a deep vein of introversion. When we arrived in London, my three cousins, my three siblings, and I were pushed outside and told to play. But we did not play. Instead, we all sat there like lumps—all of us immobile.

We sat on the concrete driveway with our hands in our laps, not saying a word. Staring at each other. Shy. No developed social graces. After an interminably long wait, some brave one of us would mumble that we should play a game. Then, for a short span of time, we had riotous fun—only to be piled back in the station wagon for the long drive home. Too soon.

To this day, when I am feeling overwhelmed by a social situation, I think, "Don't be a lump, Colleen."

23

During library time, I was devoted to checking out two book series: *Mrs. Piggle-Wiggle* by Betty MacDonald and *Pippi Longstocking* by Astrid Lindgren.

The main character of *Mrs. Piggle-Wiggle* is an older woman who lives in an upside-down house. The plot of each book is essentially the same: Mrs. Piggle Wiggle helps a child overcome a bad habit. In one book, a child won't pick up toys. Mrs. Piggle Wiggle uses magic to cure the child's messiness. In another, a child interrupts, so the magic cure is that every time the child interrupts he goes mute. Mrs. Piggle-Wiggle is never judgmental and unfailingly kind. In retrospect, I am pretty sure I read *Mrs. Piggle-Wiggle* to get reassurance that the world was an ordered, friendly place.

In contrast, disorder reigns in *Pippi Longstocking* novels. The character of Pippi Longstocking is similar to Peter Pan: she is a child who does not want to grow up or live by the conventions imposed on children. Pippi lives with a monkey and a horse, wears what she wants, stretches the truth often, has an explosive temper, and a kind heart. Although only nine years old, Pippi is independent: she has no parents (mom died and dad is a lost sea captain). She also has a suitcase full of gold coins. Pippi speaks with confidence, saying, "Don't you worry about me. I'll always come out on top." The plot of each Pippi Longstocking book is roughly the same: An adventure during which adults want Pippi to conform, and she does not. Her imagination and lack of manners survive untainted. I am not exactly sure why I read Pippi Longstocking books. Pippi scared me, but she also fascinated me.

In grade school, I was a well-behaved child. Quietly obedient. Chris probably considered me revoltingly good. He disliked that I always did the right thing. I did not always do the right thing but almost always. Chris did not always do the right thing. Kindergarten Chris had outbursts in the toy aisle of the grocery store. Chris would plant himself in front of the toys and refuse to leave unless Mom bought him a toy. If Mom chose

not to buy Chris a new toy, she carried a kicking, crying, and screaming
Chris out of the store. Grocery mission abandoned. Often, Mom simply
let Chris get a toy. An arrangement that worked for them. Every time
Chris arrived home with a new toy, Dad would shake his head and
sometimes say to Chris, "You should be more like Colleen."

Dad's words did not help our sibling relationship. I did not find Chris
revoltingly bad. On the contrary, I was jealous. Insanely so. Chris lived a
Pippi Longstocking existence: an adventurous nonconformist, going after
what he wanted. I lived a Mrs. Piggle-Wiggle life: a quiet do-gooder who
loved books. Brainwashed.

24

We drove to Virginia Beach, Virginia—our first weeklong vacation
as a family. A vacation vacation. Not a vacation to see relatives. Dad
was driving, smoking in the car as usual. One Marlboro cigarette after
another. Windows up. We had to be very careful not to touch the back of
Dad's seat. That set him off.

The car ride was going well. Jane even started singing. Jane didn't belt
out the words. She whispered the lyrics. I had to lean in to hear her.
She was singing *Greensleeves*:

Alas, my love, you do me wrong,
To cast me off discourteously.
For I have loved you well and long,
Delighting in your company.
Greensleeves was all my joy
Greensleeves was my delight,
Greensleeves was my heart of gold,
And who but my lady Greensleeves.
Dad, perhaps out of boredom, said, "What are you singing, Jane?"
"Greensleeves."
"Do you want to be a singer someday?"

"I don't know."
"Well, let's see if you have what it takes. Sing louder so I can hear you."
Jane upped her volume and gave it her best shot.
"Alas, my love, you do me wrong,
To cast me off discourteously.
For I have loved you well and long,
Delighting in your company.
Greensleeves…."

Dad, interrupted Jane mid-song and said, "Nope, you do not have what it takes."

We all stayed quiet the remainder of the drive to Virginia.

25

I liked child actor Haley Mills. She was best known for the movie *The Parent Trap*, but I loved her most in *The Trouble with Angels*, a movie about two rebellious girls getting into scrape after scrape in an all-girls Catholic boarding school.

Heck, I was a Catholic girl growing up in Michigan. Very relatable. Haley Mill's character Mary Clancey has a tagline sentence that she says many times in the movie: "I've got the most scathingly brilliant idea!" I loved the way Haley Mills uttered that sentence. Every time. I totally believed her—over and over again.

Inspired, Tilda and I wanted to do something scathingly brilliant. We decided to chew the same piece of gum for the entire school year. Tilda had her piece of gum. I had mine. September to June.

At night, we placed the gum in a sealed baby food jar that each of us kept bedside. We were allowed to add a speck or two of fresh gum to restore the flavor. Only as needed. Chiclets tiny size gum worked well.

If the wad of gum grew too big, we were allowed to cut it down to a manageable size. While our classmates were grossed out, there was an edge of respect and envy in their disgust. Tilda and I remained focused and accomplished our goal.

On the first day of summer, Tilda and I ceremoniously buried the hard, gray wads of chewing gum in her backyard garden. We used the baby food jars as coffins.

26

Dad and Mom offered heavy-handed parental coaching on the importance of good manners, especially preceding any visit to relatives: Sit still with your hands in your lap and be quiet. Good posture was also mandated. Jennifer, Jane, Chris, and I tried hard to be good. Almost always.

On a trip to New Brunswick we were scheduled to meet my great grandmother. She was in her nineties at the time. At the motel, my mother had us scrub ourselves clean and put on our Sunday best. Matching plaid jumpers, ankle socks, and black buckle shoes for the girls. Chris wore dress slacks and a blue shirt—his hair slicked back with a touch of hair tonic.

Upon arrival to Great Grandmother's house, we were ushered into a formal living room where the four of us sat rigidly straight on a long couch with our hands in our laps waiting to meet Great Grandmother. After just a few minutes, my great grandmother's wheelchair was pushed into the room by a caregiver. It took a few moments for me to realize she was completely blind. No one thought to explain this to the children before the visit. I guess Dad and Mom thought it impolite to mention. After introductions, we sat while the adults talked.

I was scared because I was scared of almost everything. Blindness ranked an 8 or 9 on my fear scale. I sat there trying to imagine what my great grandmother saw instead of sight. I had it in my head that she most likely saw a wall of blackness or maybe perpetual redness—like the inside of my eyelids when the sun shone on my face and my eyes were closed.

While I sat there thinking my thoughts, Jane had other things going on, namely balking at the need to sit up straight and tolerate tight, uncomfortable shoes when our great grandmother could not even see our politeness. Jane slumped down on the couch and pushed the heels of her shoes off, letting them dangle on her toes over the wood floor. Flirting with danger. Across the room, my parents were throwing severe you-better-cut-it-out looks at Jane. Then, in desperation, they graduated to their wait-until-we-get-in-the-car looks. At some point, one of Jane's shoes dropped to the wood floor with a loud thud. Without hesitation, Great Grandmother looked blindly but directly at Jane and said in a steely tone, "You should mind your manners, Jane."

I was no longer scared. I was terrified. How did Great Grandmother know it was Jane? She's blind. My brain immediately and frantically concluded, "She's a witch!" I wet my pants. Politely and quietly.

Jane did not get in trouble for testing the waters of rudeness that day. Instead, during the car ride back to the motel, all discussion was about my lack of bladder control and the sizeable wet spot left on the antique Chesterfield. I learned Dad had a predilection: To him, every couch was a Chesterfield, whether it was a Chesterfield or not.

27

School lunch was served in the gymnasium where Murphy-bed-style tables were pulled down from the walls midday and then folded back-up by Mrs. Jones and crew, readied for afternoon PE classes.

Tilda had a knack for getting in trouble. She was glamorous in that way. She said things that should be left unsaid. She did things that should be left undone. She knew adults were humans with vulnerabilities before any of her age-mates realized the same. She was funny. Really funny. I ate lunch with Tilda every day, honored to share a seat at her table.

For most students, lunchtime did not come with an edge of mystery. Lunch bag packing was adult business, a task done without consultation. Predictable. Repetitive. Across the gymnasium, students unfolded their brown bags each day knowing what they would find inside. Bologna on Wonder Bread with ketchup. A sandwich all of us tolerated, without complaint. We would smash our side bags of potato chips and pour the crumbs on top of the bologna. The chips gave the sandwich a crunchy palatability.

Tilda's lunch bag contents, however, defied the ordinary. She had a peanut butter and jelly sandwich and chips along with Pop-Tarts or a double-pack of Twinkies, sometimes both, day after day. We imagined she had the best mom on the planet. One day though Tilda unpacked her lunch and found a surprise: Bologna on Wonder Bread with ketchup. For a second, she was one of us. Maybe half a second.

Tilda quickly grabbed the circle of bologna and with great disgust threw it under the lunch table. Shocked, my tablemates and I stared. Tilda casually proceeded to eat her ketchup, potato chip, and Wonder Bread sandwich minus bologna. It was hard not to feel inadequate in the presence of her genius. We had never thought a bologna rebellion was on the table or, in this case, under the table.

At the end of lunch, Mrs. Jones, the lunch lady, came around to dismiss tables one-by-one. She checked to make sure our garbage was thrown away, nothing on or under each table. When she arrived at our table, we were nearly dismissed when Mrs. Jones spotted Tilda's circle of bologna stuck to the floor under the table. She asked, "Whose bologna is on the floor?"

Mrs. Jones dismissed each student who said, "Not mine, Mrs. Jones," until only two students remained: Tilda and me. It was not my bologna, but I was a little scared of both Tilda and Mrs. Jones. I remained silent.

Not having time to solve the crime, Mrs. Jones said, "You two will stay after to sweep the floor." Once the tables were tucked away in the walls, Tilda and I were handed two giant, industrial brooms. As Mrs. Jones exited the gym, she sternly told us we had fifteen minutes to get the floors cleaned up for afternoon gym classes.

As we swept, Tilda began singing the lyrics to Billy Rico's "Me and Mrs. Jones," using her broom handle as microphone.

"Me and Mrs. Jones
We got a thing goin' on
We both know that it's wrong
But it's much too strong
To let it go now"

Tilda and I giggled and swept. The emptiness of the space amplified Tilda's voice. She kept belting out, "Me and Mrs. Jones, Mrs. Jones, Mrs. Jones." And I kept begging her to quiet down, even though I did not want her to stop.

28

At the end of the school year, the entire 6th grade attended Camp Tamarack. A week or two before the trip, students were asked to submit the names of classmates they wanted as bunkmates. The camp housing was divided into several bunkhouses— a boys' section and a girls' section. Students were placed in groups of two for bunk bed sharing and assigned a bunkhouse of twelve students for communal living. Each bunkhouse was a team, eating together, attending activities together, and hanging out together. I wrote down the names of my two closest friends: Debbie and Tilda. Debbie, Tilda, and I lived on the same block and walked to school together every day. A day or two later, camping assignments were posted. Debbie and Tilda were listed as bunk bed partners. I was the odd person out. Not even placed in the same bunkhouse. The curse of a three-friend group.

I was partnered with a new girl: Lucy. I immediately guessed why I was partnered with Lucy. I was kind. Teachers thought that if anyone would buddy up with Lucy, it was Colleen. Colleen the doormat. In my mind, my teachers stuck me with Lucy because I would not complain.

I felt the first outrage of my life. My teachers imagined I would suck up my profound disappointment and behave well. I did not. I waged a war of rebellion. The entire week at Camp Tamarack, I did not speak to my bunkmate Lucy. Not even once. My teacher Mr. Slater pulled me aside and told me how disappointed he was in me. I didn't care. I was disappointed in him. I remained silent and sullen for the full week. Lucy represented all the injustice in the world.

I owe Lucy an apology.

29

I broke the law. Nothing dramatic, but still a legal indiscretion.

Once. Only once. Breaking and entering. "The criminal act of entering a residence or other enclosed property through the slightest amount of force, without authorization." Tilda convinced me to break into a neighbor's garage. "Mrs. Waterson is batty," Tilda argued. "She'll never even know." Tilda loved the word batty. And she called anyone she disliked a hot bat. It sounded pretty cool when Tilda said it. And when mad or happy, depending on the circumstance, Tilda put *hot* in front of *damn*. Hot damn. Her delivery was enviable.

Tilda told me that there was something she had to show me. Tilda begged, "Pleeeease." She promised I'd be glad I did it. I reasoned that the garage was a good distance from the main house and Tilda was my best friend. Maybe my only real friend. I caved.

Tilda knew exactly which of Mrs. Waterson's garage windows was unlocked. An easy point of entry. We climbed in. I looked around. There were rows and rows of brown boxes. Tilda whispered, "Come here." She opened one of the boxes. I squealed in delight when I saw the contents. The box contained a pristine stack of *National Geographic* magazines. Every box in the garage contained *National Geographic* magazines in mint condition. Hundreds. That summer I became a juvenile delinquent. Tilda and I visited the Waterson garage nearly every day to read and look at pictures.

Before opening each magazine, I ran my hand across the smooth cover. A magical feeling—perhaps not worth jail time, but close. The statute of limitations on breaking and entering is six to ten years.

30

"Mom, May I go to Tilda's house?

"No."

"No" was almost always the answer. My dad and Tilda's dad fought over our apple tree. Once a week during mowing season. Tilda's dad complained that the apples that fell from our apple tree mucked up his riding mower. Tilda's family owned the big field that ran behind all the houses on our block. Three sides of the block were modest homes, starter homes. Tilda's house occupied the remaining side of the block. A circle drive. Two tree houses. A tennis court. A pool. A pontoon boat. Her parents even had separate bedrooms.

I was pleasantly surprised when I next asked Mom what seemed to me a dream to be soon denied, "Mom, may I sleep over Tilda's house on Friday?"

"Yes, Farris and I have a wedding."

"We are going to sleep outside in a tent."

"Be sure you take blankets. And be good."

"I will."

Friday came. After dinner I changed into my elephant bell jeans, a T-shirt, and a red sweatshirt. My elephant bell jeans were not just flared a little at the bottom but had a huge flare. The only trendy pair of clothing I possessed. I wore my elephant bells self-consciously. They were a little tight. Passed down to me from Jane.

On our block, all houses ate dinner at 5:30 p.m. After dinner, all children six years or older were kicked outside to play. Children who were allowed to play with Tilda met on her tennis court. When I arrived, I was relieved to see Tilda had also worn her elephant bell jeans. Hers were super-sized elephant bells.

Our sleepover started with a neighborhood game of dodgeball. The net was down, so the playing surface was expansive. Tennis court dodgeball was simple. Equipment: Kickball. Teams: No teams. Object: Every person tried to stay alive, dodging the ball when thrown by another player. Winner: The last player remaining. When the game progressed to only six players remaining, the playing surface was reduced to half-court.

The game began. Three older boys in the neighborhood were playing. Middle school boys. The rest of us were in elementary school. The boys were nice but played to win. I was out quickly. It took a while for the game to get down to six players. When the seventh player was eliminated, the six remaining players shifted to half-court. Tilda was still in. The only girl. Two 5th grade boys and three middle school boys were still in. The middle school boys decided to form a temporary alliance. They quickly eliminated the younger boys. Tilda remained. The odds were stacked against her. Brutally so. But she was never one to quit.

Tilda impressively dodged a few throws leveled in her direction. Then, one of the boys threw a ball that clipped the material of Tilda's super-sized elephant bells.

"You're out!" the three middle school boys screamed in unison.

"Elephant bells don't count," Tilda retorted with attitude. The attitude of a property owner.

Tilda's stubbornness was well known. Arguing with her was pointless. She owned the tennis court. The three middle school boys quit. They walked away. So did the rest of the neighborhood. Tilda won. The victory did not make Tilda happy. She was focused on revenge against the three boys who were, in her words, "babyfide quitters."

I followed Tilda back to the tent. As I arranged my bed, Tilda retrieved a brick of firecrackers from her duffle. "What are you going to do with those?" I questioned.

"When it gets pitch black outside, I am going to light a firecracker on the porch of each babyfide loser."

"I am not allowed to play with firecrackers."

"You do not have to go with me, but I want you to listen to the three booms." Tilda and I talked and ate snacks until late into the night. I was tired. Tilda was wide awake. Revenge adrenaline. She pulled on a black sweatshirt. She departed with a small flashlight, three firecrackers, and a silver lighter. Her silver lighter was just like the one my dad used to light his Marlboro cigarettes.

I waited in the tent. Scared. Scared to be alone in the dark. Tilda left me alone in a tent in the middle of the night. Abandoned.

I heard the first BOOM. A few minutes later, a second BOOM. Finally, a third BOOM. There was silence, then angry shouts into the night. I waited anxiously for Tilda. I heard sirens in the distance, gradually getting louder. Getting closer.

The tent flap ripped open. Tilda dove in—with wild eyes and victory-fueled laughter. She whispered, "Hot damn. I did it." She looked over at me and smiled. It was hard not to admire Tilda's courage and accomplishment. Even if vengeful and illegal.

We both snuggled into our blankets. Exhausted.

31

I didn't choose my brother Chris. And he didn't choose me. I should have been better. I wasn't.

We were on yet another road trip from Detroit to New Brunswick. Relatives, again. A sixteen-hour and forty-two-minute drive. One thousand twenty-nine miles. We still had a station wagon. And, no surprise, Chris and I were put in the third seat again, mostly out of ear shot of my parents. But not out of range of Dad's thick cigarette smoke. A two-pack a day habit. One cigarette after another. No cracked window for fresh air.

On this car ride, Chris was the victim of my boredom. Before we were even out of Michigan, I told Chris I could make him smile just by staring at him. I told him I had mind control abilities. I told him he was powerless. I stared at him. And stared at him. He whispered, "Stop it." I knew he was cracking. I kept staring. And staring, saying, "You will smile. You are in my control." At this point in the road trip. Chris and I were having what might be termed confusing fun. Eventually he smiled. I won. In retaliation, Chris started a stealth campaign of invasion.

The upholstered car seats had heavy stitched lines, providing a neat linear boundary. A thick center stitch became the Maginot Line between my territory and his territory. Separate lands provided a measure of peace. After Chris lost the smiling game, however, he boldly put the tip of his finger over the stitched centerline and waited for me to notice. When I did notice, I tried to grab his finger. Not successful. He kept it up. Every time I failed to grab his finger, he giggled. I did not find the invasion of my territory humorous. After many repeated attempts, I was finally able to capture his finger and crush it in my grip. When Chris seemed just on the verge of crying, I let go.

Confusing fun had now transitioned to mean fun. While I was able to thwart Chris's assault on my space, I felt Chris needed an additional reminder of my superiority. My age advantage was unfair, but effective. Psychological warfare. My forte. As we continued our journey to New Brunswick, I noticed that Canada had many gas stations named with big BP signs. The British Petroleum Company was not really a Michigan thing in the 1970s. I am not even sure there were BP gas stations in the United States back then. I knew Chris was unfamiliar with BP gas stations.

My new game was simple: I watched the passing landscape with radar precision. Every time I saw a BP gas station, I mumbled BP ten times in quick succession in a monotone, trance-like voice—just loud enough for Chris to hear. I did not make eye contact with Chris. I continued this strategy for the remainder of the car ride to New Brunswick. To his credit, Chris was toughening up. He ignored me.

When our week-long visit with relatives was over, we loaded back into the station wagon. Our New Brunswick to Detroit journey commenced. As soon as we passed the first BP gas station, I reengaged in battle: "BP, BP, BP, BP, BP, BP, BP, BP, BP, BP." Chris, exhausted from the trip, begged me for silence. I negotiated with him, "If you can figure out what I am saying and why I am saying it, I'll stop." After about five more BP, BP, BP, BP, BP, BP, BP, BP, BP, BP campaigns, Chris cracked. He kicked me. Dad noticed. Chris was scolded. I smiled. Victory.

My misdeeds were most likely caused by the inhalation of cigarette smoke. Dad's fault.

32

Halloween was magical. Jennifer was brilliant at dreaming up ideas and executing her ideas. She once cut old white sheets into strips and spatter-painted each strip with a varying amount of red. On Halloween evening, Jennifer, dressed in white tights and white t-shirt, tied the faux-bloody strips from head-to-toe, making the most authentic mummy costume, a Lon Chaney transformation. Another year, she and two girlfriends tie-dyed three sheets, sewed them together, and created a three-headed monster get-up. Jennifer was Halloween cool.

We had recently moved to a new neighborhood—away from Tilda. Jennifer had not yet had time to make friends, so she invited me into her web of costume-making. I was thrilled. We decided to make ragdoll costumes. Spooky ragdoll costumes. We purchased yarn skeins and spent a week making ragdoll wigs. We found white pinafores to go over our school dresses, making them doll dresses. We pinned spiders, bats, and sequins on the pinafores to create an eerie effect. By Halloween, we were ready.

We went out into the neighborhood. Knocked on the first door. "Trick-or-treat!" Candy dropped in our bags and costume compliments were given. Jennifer and I were giggling, beaming, bonding. Second house. "Trick-or-treat!" Full-sized candy bars were dropped in our bags. Generous treats and again costume praise. Jennifer and I ran breathlessly to the third house and laugh-yelled, "Trick-or-Treat!"

A woman answered the door. She surveyed our costumes and then looked directly at Jennifer. She said in a judgmental tone, "Aren't you a little too old to be out trick-or-treating?" Jennifer, immediately self-conscious, grabbed my arm and yanked me off the doorstep. We walked home in silence. Jennifer was crying. The only thing worse than having a perfect older sister is seeing that perfect older sister cry.

Halloween ended after only three houses. I spent the rest of the evening passing out candy to disappointed children who came trick-or-treating to my house. Mom had purchased a bulk-sized box of root beer barrel hard candies for distribution. Not a crowd favorite. More trick than treat.

33

My best nonhuman friend in elementary and middle school was a volume of *Grimm's Fairy Tales*. The stories were darker than Disney movies but still filled with princesses and princes.

My new best human friend was Edie Taft, a girl who lived three houses down the street from my new house. I recently began to doubt the existence of true love. I was not going to ask my mom about love. She was the person who gave me the fairy tale book. I knew her position: A prince will someday show up.

Edie had an approachable mom. One day, Edie went upstairs to get something. My opportune moment presented itself: I was alone with Mrs. Taft. I quickly stammered three big questions at Mrs. Taft: "Is true love real?" "Am I going to meet someone someday who will know that we are meant to be together?" "Is it all a lie?"

It should be noted that before this three-question moment, I had never said more than a respectful hello or good-bye to Mrs. Taft. I remember Mrs. Taft looking momentarily shocked by my sudden outburst, but she answered with a shrug, "There is love. It is hard, but sort of magical. I suppose."

This was not definitive reassurance. The "I suppose" unsettled me. My eyes filled with tears. Mrs. Taft, quickly redirected our conversation— asked me if I'd like Chinese takeout for dinner and yelled to Edie, "Edieeeeeeeee, come downstairs now, please!"

34

Soon after we moved, Chris invented a new game for us to play. He'd say, "Do you want to spy?" I always nodded yes. We'd find what we thought was a clever place to hide and observe a sister or two—unbeknownst to them. Usually belly-down behind a couch or around a corner. The game ended when we were caught.

Once we had the idea to go into my sister Jane's closet when her bedroom was empty and wait. Her slotted closet door provided adequate cover and a clear view. The wait was thrilling. My brother and I practiced extreme control—no giggles, no elbow jabs, no noise of any kind.

Eventually Jane entered her room. Jane threw herself in her under-stuffed, uncomfortable beanbag chair and started reading her go-to-book: *The Last of the Mohicans*. Jane was always reading *The Last of the Mohicans*. We quietly observed her reading, but she heard a noise from the closet. Chris and I may have been breathing too loudly. Jane screamed a bloodcurdling scream. Mom and Dad came running. Jane pointed to the closet. Dad yanked open the closet door. Game over.

Jane was seriously rattled, though she quickly shifted to older sister outrage, accusing us of invasion of privacy. Chris and I argued that we did not mean to scare Jane or find out any secrets. We were just playing a game. Argument rejected. Chris and I were punished. Not allowed to leave the yard for a week.

35

In middle school I rebelled against my given name. I thought Colleen
was too plain. Girl plain.

I started spelling Colleen differently. My teen brain thought Collene was
more beautiful than Colleen. And sometimes I would purposely drop one
l, signing my tests and quizzes Coleen. No one noticed. Two l's and
two e's seemed superfluous. No easy escape exists from Colleen.
No ready nickname.

I decided to go counterculture. I stubbornly insisted my family and
friends call me Neelloc. Colleen spelled backwards. The Neelloc phase
lasted only two weeks, because it coincided with my reading of
The Time Machine by H.G. Wells. In the novel, there are creatures who
live underground called Morlocks. Neelloc. Morlock. Too close. I wanted
to be a rebel, not a monster. Roughly about the same time, I read *Romeo
and Juliet* and was introduced to the whole a rose by any other name
would smell as sweet argument. I did not buy in. Juliet Capulet. Colleen
Capulet. Nope—did not smell as sweet.

Colleen, however, was better than my last name: Elgee. Pronounced L-G.
Colleen Elgee. How many e's is one person supposed to endure? My
friends teased me, calling me Colleen Allergy. They would fake sneeze
when I approached. It became a thing. Elgee. Allergy. Close is close
enough, I guess. The sneezes did not last forever, because my classmate
Warren soon noted that Elgee sounded like algae. Colleen Algae. Instead
of sneezing when I walked in a room, friends and nonfriends would
announce, "There is fungus among us."

Algae is not a fungus, but none of us knew that at the time.

36

In 7th grade, I enrolled in an elective course titled Genetics taught by Mrs. Carlton. Mrs. Carlton was the coolest teacher in middle school. Mrs. Carlton required that each student bring in a male and female mouse, hamster, or rabbit to care for, to breed, to study and then to write a scientific paper on the experience. Genetics was more popular than Home Economics. Live animals or cinnamon rolls? Live animals. Genetics was more popular than Gym Class. Live animals or dodge ball? Live animals. Genetics was more popular than Wood Shop. Live animals or power tools? Close. But still, live animals.

Students loved the Genetics elective, but parents did not. I remember the hesitation in my dad's approval when I asked to bring my mice home for Winter Break. I was allowed to keep the mice in our unfinished basement. My mice family, the mouse parents and six offspring, liked their new surroundings. In fact, four of them escaped their aquarium enclosure to go exploring. My fault. I neglected to secure the screen lid after a feeding. I could not tell Jennifer or Jane about the escape. Only Chris could keep a secret involving fugitive rodents. He was good like that.

Stealthily, Chris and I spent hours trying to catch the errant mice using a G.I. Joe cast net and a large Styrofoam mountain from our Lionel train set. We successfully captured three of the four escapees. My brother and I surmised that the other mouse must have somehow tunneled outdoors. Two weeks later, a scream from the kitchen signaled an error in our hypothesis. After listening to my tearful confession, my parents determined my punishment: four consecutive weekends of yardwork. A bogus sentence.

I did not end up becoming a geneticist or pest control executive, but the learning from that elective class stuck. I still remember, with clarity, our study of Gregor Mendel, Mendelian Inheritance, dominant and recessive phenotypes, Punnett squares, and Drosophila melanogaster.

37

My mom drove me back to the old neighborhood to spend a Friday with Tilda. Later that night, Tilda's mom drove Tilda and me to The Rink. Three hours of roller skating: 6-9. Tilda was an expert at roller skating. She owned skates. And practiced on her circle drive. I rented skates. Ugly brown and orange skates. I was not expert level, but I was at least intermediate level.

Tilda and I had three hours of reminiscing and skating. A few minutes before closing time, the rink manager announced that all skaters must be picked up by 9:15 p.m. The doors would be locked at 9:15 p.m. Me being me, I caught up to Tilda on the skating floor and asked her when our ride was coming.

"We do not have a ride. We need to find one," replied Tilda casually.

When the skating session ended, I returned my skates. Tilda stood in line for a slushie. I was frantic.

"Tilda, should we call your mom?"

"No."

We went outside The Rink. Tilda worked the crowd. She soon yelled, "Colleen, get over here," as she loaded herself in a purple van. A van with psychedelic detailing. I jumped in rather than be left behind. I sat in a vacant seat. The van driver and his friends seemed nice but scary. All boys. Older. Long hair.

The driver announced the side van door would remain open as we drove. He needed fresh air. The van smelled like something I smelled once at an Elton John concert that I was forced to go to with Jennifer. I thought I was going to be ill. I thought Tilda and I were in big trouble. Kidnapped even.

I immediately started saying the Our Father over and over. Mentally begging God to spare my life. And Tilda's.

"What are you saying?" shouted Tilda.

"Prayers."

Tilda laughed. Her hair blew in the wind coming from the open door. She looked alive. Happy. I am quite sure we were over the speed limit.

We made it safely home. I kissed the ground at Tilda's house.

38

I could have easily been the target of meanness, especially in 8th grade. I only owned one pair of pants. And not jeans. My pants were an emerald-green polyester blend. Not okay. I had to wear the same green pants to school every day. Monday. Tuesday. Wednesday. Thursday. Friday. Also, I let my sister Jane cut my hair. Surprisingly, it turned out okay. Two days later, however, we were bored, and she cut my hair again. It did not turn out okay. For whatever reason, in my neighborhood in Michigan during the 1970s, a live and let live spirit reigned, even at school. I was never bullied.

Have I ever been the bully? Guilty of habitual meanness toward another? Maybe. Chris and I did not hang out anymore. He was in elementary school and I was in middle school. In the upstairs of our house, more than once, I blocked the hallway so Chris could not get to his bedroom. I rationalized: It was a game. And then there was the time Chris was walking by me in our front yard. I threw a football at his back for no good reason. After a heavy, wet snowfall, Chris built a magnificent snowman in our backyard. When he went in the house for lunch, I pushed the head off his snowman. I was careful to destroy the evidence of my boot prints. I never claimed responsibility, but Chris knew when our eyes met. I quietly repented after the decapitation. A step too far.

Why did I do these things? I honestly don't know. Maybe my self-imposed embarrassment caused by having one pair of green pants, a Jane haircut, and other middle school stressors fueled my bouts of cruelty. Whatever the reason, even if my actions are forgiven, I still feel guilt.

39

Chris and I went to the movies together: 1976, *King Kong*. It was holiday break, and I wanted to see the remake of *King Kong*. Chris wanted popcorn. Our worlds intersected. Like old times.

The plot of *King Kong* contains no surprises: Greedy members of a corporation are on a boat are looking for oil in the Indian Ocean. A shipwreck occurs. The survivors end up on an island, including the beautiful female protagonist Dwan, specifically not Dawn, played by actor Jessica Lange. The inhabitants of the island live behind a large wall to protect themselves from a creature called Kong. Kong is a giant ape. Dwan is given to Kong as a sacrifice. Kong falls in love with Dwan. Kong is captured and taken to New York and put on display. Kong escapes. Kong reunites with Dwan. Kong climbs a tall building. Kong is attacked by helicopters and flamethrowers. Kong falls. Dwan is safe. Kong dies.

A predictable storyline—except there was a surprise. Kong's death destroyed me. As the movie ended, I sat crying uncontrollably in the dark theatre. Chris was mortified.

When the lights came up in the theatre, he said, "I'll wait outside."

40

I have a retrospective love of Valentine's Day, especially the class parties. Every year at school, until 6th grade, students made Valentine mailboxes out of shoeboxes. Boxes of Valentine cards had no duplicates, no commercialized themes. Every card had different artwork. And a different saying.

It was fun to read all the cards and then match each card with a classmate. In 6th grade, I had just enough cards for the number of students in my class. Problem: One of the cards had a football player on it that read "Be on my team, Valentine!" "A little forward," I thought. The card caused me emotional distress, but I caved to the thrill of Valentine's Day. Its promise of love. I ended up giving the football player card to a boy named Craig. Frankly, I did not even know if I liked Craig. He just seemed nicer and quieter than all the other boys. The class Valentine's party came and went without Craig mentioning my card. Whew. That year, I loved every card I received. Unrequited love was not even a blip on my radar screen.

By 7th grade, just one year later, Valentine's Day had lost its childish joy. If possible, I was even more self-conscious. And I was for the first time aware, if not hyper-aware, of the social world at school. I did not understand it, but I was aware of it. At the junior high Valentine's dance, a classmate named Mike said to me, "You tried too hard match your clothes?" I was stunned and hurt. I was wearing black slacks, white blouse, black sweater and black-white Oxford shoes. Mike was right, but his criticism pained me for days afterward. Even years afterward.

Then there was a big boy-girl party held at Tom's house. While 7th grade seems too early for romance, the beginnings of figuring out how to like and love were there. Brutally there. Romance at a most unromantic time. I begged Mom to go to Tom's party. Everyone was going. She predictably said, "No." The Monday after the big party was a lonely day for me at school.

In 7th grade, I met a boy named Jim. He lived in the subdivision adjacent to my subdivision. He delivered the newspaper to our house. He mowed our lawn. Dad would get furious when Jim scalped the hills of our front yard landscaping with his mower. Jim whistled. Really well. I liked to listen to him whistle.

41

The summer of 1976 ranks as a retrospectively great summer. I did not have a personality. Still quaking with self-consciousness. But I had Edie as my friend, so I tried on her interests.

Edie was baseball crazy. Detroit Tiger pitcher Mark "The Bird" Fidrych pitched his rookie season with the Detroit Tigers in 1976. Fidrych was known not only for prodigy-level pitching, but also for his odd behavior—he strutted, he talked to the ball, he didn't like the groundskeepers touching his pitching mound during a game. And he looked like Big Bird. He was captivatingly odd. That summer, whenever Mark Fidrych had an autograph signing event, Edie and I were in line. We met Fidrych countless times. Edie had a crush on him. She had pictures of Fidrych that filled half the walls of her pink bedroom. My mom didn't allow me to use tape on my bedroom walls. But my mom did allow me sign-up for a summer softball league with Edie. Mrs. Taft volunteered to do all the driving.

The other half of Edie's bedroom was filled with pictures of a band called The Bay City Rollers—a pop singing group. The Bay City Rollers were five guys from Scotland who always wore plaid: Eric, Stuart, Les, Alan, and Derek. Their biggest hit was titled "Saturday Night." My memory of the song is that the band yell-spells S-A-T-U-R-D-A-Y and the scream-sings "Night!" Over and over. Edie was in love with the band member named Stuart, nicknamed "Woody," because, Edie said, "Woody is misunderstood." I was never too big on the boy band craze, nor did I like plaid all that much. I sort of fake-crushed on Derek, the band's drummer. It felt silly.

The next summer or maybe it was the next, next summer, we shifted to loving the singer Meat Loaf. Really, we just loved one song: "Two Out of Three Ain't Bad." We built a whole summer around that one song. Edie and I sat in her bedroom and belted the song out thousands of times. We recorded ourselves and giggled when we messed up. I cannot sing. But somehow Edie and I did not care about that. We felt what mattered was simply being 100% invested in the vocals, in feeling the lyrics. Like Meat Loaf.

We thought one verse was the pinnacle of brilliant song writing:

"You'll never find your gold on a sandy beach
You'll never drill for oil on a city street
I know you're looking for a ruby in a mountain of rocks
But there ain't no Coup de Ville hiding at the bottom
Of a Cracker Jack box"

Edie taught me that loving something, anything could be an all-in, cover your bedroom walls state-of-being.

To this day, whenever I am driving on a long road trip and the whole car is asleep, I sing "Two Out of Three Ain't Bad." I still know every word. I don't sing it loud, but just loud enough to recapture the feeling of that summer. I softly sang this same song to my children when they were babies to help them get to sleep. A Meat Loaf lullaby.

42

As a teen, I lacked an awareness of basic hygiene. I spent my time reading and imagining. Who dreamed about shampoo and soap? I never gave them a thought. I still lived with the brave knights and the princesses in my books.

As middle school unfolded, I slowly became more aware of the real world. And my place in it. At some point, a moment of self-awareness came as an epiphany. A frantic moment of cruddy clarity: I needed a shower. My hair was greasy.

I jumped in a hot shower, shampooing twice, lathering-rinsing-repeating, with my dad's Head and Shoulders and then conditioning my hair with my mother's Faberge Organics Conditioner.

My dad had an unopened Aqua Velva soap-on-a-rope from Father's Day a few years back. It became mine.

43

I had an existential crisis in literature class. I was introduced to the poem *Ulysses* by Tennyson.

To simplify, the poem's title character—an aging hero—wants to go on one last sailing adventure:

"And this gray spirit yearning in desire
To follow knowledge like a sinking star,
Beyond the utmost bounds of human thought"

My teen brain started thinking. If Ulysses sails towards the horizon will he ever reach the horizon? No. The horizon will remain always a horizon. Never an achieved end. Merely the illusion of forward movement toward a horizon never to be reached.

Infinity. All over again. I tried not to think about it.

44

I loved noon guitar-Mass more than regular morning Mass. Guitar-Mass felt happy. Dad and Mom preferred to go earlier in the day.

On an unusual Sunday, Mom and I were the only ones attending Mass, and we were going to noon Mass, guitar-Mass. Happiness. Now that Jennifer and Jane were in high school and had high school homework, all-family Mass attendance waned. Dad and Chris often stayed home, too.

We arrived at church with only a few minutes to spare, so the pews were nearly full. My mom and I slid into a back pew. I was excited. Once settled, I immediately grabbed the missal and hunkered down to read. I preferred to read rather than listen to the priest's sermon. Probably a sin. I did perk up to say the Our Father, to sing hymns, to listen to gospel readings, and to shake hands and say, "Peace be with you." And I loved when our priest chanted in a beautiful voice, "Through Him, with Him and in Him, in the unity of the Holy Spirit, all glory and honor is yours, almighty Father, for ever and ever."

This particular Saturday, Mom and I did not stay for the Eucharist Prayer though. After the Mass readings, the priest explained how the day's readings applied to everyday life. I was not listening. I was still reading the stories in the missal. But something strange happened. Sounds of sadness happened. I looked up. Not one but about thirty women exited the church crying. In the middle of Mass. I was confused and upset. I asked, "Mom, what is happening?" No answer.

Mom took my hand, and we left Mass with the crying women. When we were in the car, Mom explained, "The priest talked about a topic that hurt the souls of women. It is something you would not understand." Mom never went back to Mass. We became non-practicing Catholics.

It wasn't until I was in my thirties that Mom shared the topic of the priest's sermon: the position of the Catholic Church on contraceptives.

45

In high school, I was required to take swimming class. Big groan. I was not a good swimmer. I could make it from one side of the Olympic-size pool to the other. Not pretty. Not without internal panic. My swim teacher Coach Kerr had a notoriously demanding coaching style, loudly nurturing gradual skill building and individual accountability.

During class, Coach Kerr barked high praise or barked correction. She'd shout a swimmer's last name and a word or two. "Smith, excellent form." "McAllister, messy work." "Kincaid, what are you doing? The rest of us are doing the breaststroke."

I was more than once called out in class for my ill-executed technique. When we were practicing dives, swimmers went one-by-one to the end of the diving board. Upon the completion of each dive came Coach Kerr's assessment. After my first dive, Coach Kerr shouted, "Elgee, that is exactly how not to dive." My first dive was not a dive, but a belly-smacker. My next dive—while not clean—came closer to being an actual dive. Coach Kerr shouted, "Elgee, not right, but better." I beamed as if she had said, "Perfect dive."

Coach Kerr gave me a gift: I learned that the simple act of doing better feels good. Very good. I loved Coach Kerr as a swim teacher. She publicly announced failures and successes. She was honest and consistent—in criticism and in praise. I accepted both with grace. For the first time.

46

My all-girls parochial school was a basketball powerhouse of legendary proportions in the state of Michigan. My family moved the summer of my 9th grade year, so I would be transferring from the parochial school to the public high school for 10th grade.

My mom and Jane visited the public school campus to get me registered. I was not in tow. Somehow, they bumped into the Girls' Basketball Coach, Mr. Holmes. He introduced himself; they chatted. Jane told Mr. Holmes I was transferring from the local parochial school. Jane gushed to Mr. Holmes about me being the most athletic person in our family. This may have been true because we had no athletes in the family. Jane also tells people that I am the blond of the family. My hair is brown. Mr. Holmes shared that basketball try-outs were the next day and extended an invitation for me to come.

I picked up my first basketball ever at basketball tryouts. To begin the tryout, the coaches yelled, "Line up on the baseline."

I thought, "Baseline?" Despite my lack of skill, knowledge, and experience, I tried my best. I didn't know any better. Two days of tryouts. When I looked at the white sheet of paper taped to the gymnasium door, I learned I had made the cut. I was on the basketball team.

It wasn't until a year later that Mr. Holmes told me that he had expected a top-notch player to show up to try-outs, and then I showed up. Clueless. I asked why he gave me a spot on the team.

Mr. Holmes said he only needed eight skilled players to win games. The last two players needed to add something other than skill. He said I had heart, and I kept him humble.

47

Tilda and I reconnected in 11th grade. Like old times, Tilda invited me for a sleepover. I was hesitant, remembering The Rink incident. But Tilda had her own car now. A blue Pacer. We would not be soliciting rides from strangers.

"Mom, will you drive me to Tilda's so I can sleep over on Saturday."

"Yes." Permission granted.

Tilda and I connected as if no time had passed. She talked to me about her boyfriend and her intent to be a psychologist. I was relieved by the normalcy of it all. Later, Tilda and I hopped into her Pacer to pick up a pizza. I went inside the store to get the pizza. When I returned to the Pacer, Tilda loudly ordered, "Get in!" I did as I was told. The pizza employees inside were pointing at us. And now heading toward us.

"What is going on?!" I screamed as Tilda squealed out of the parking lot.

"I stole the gas cap off the pizza delivery car. I lost mine," Tilda explained as she tried to lose the driver of the delivery car who was on our bumper. I started saying the Our Father again. Aloud.

Tilda yelled, "Shut up!" I kept praying. Aloud. Tilda drove recklessly, risking our lives. She did lose the delivery driver, evading consequences. Tilda let out a whoop, clearly delighted with her driving skills and new gas cap.

When we were safely back at Tilda's house, I called my mom. "Mom, can you please come get me. I do not feel well."

"Yes."

48

Many significant moments of my life happened in a school hallway.
I had a new best friend at my new school. Erin and I were close. It was
a big, big school—about 1,000 students. We had lockers right next to
each other. I was awkwardly shy; Erin was outgoing. We were both
sophomores and more than a little intimidated by the throngs of
older students.

We, however, quickly made up codenames for two senior boys whom we
thought were good looking. Erin and I created alternate realities together
often. My dream guy was codenamed Kime Kurbe. We simply scrambled
letters of their real names. Remember this was the age before computers.
Erin's dream guy was K-nic Manfreed. We thought the name K-nic
particularly clever. KUH-nic, not KAY-nic. Kime and K-nic. For months,
we watched them from our lockers as they passed in the hallway, making
up stories about their lives. It was silly, but we were often silly.

One day Erin and I were standing at our lockers talking. I had my back
to the hallway. Erin suddenly grabbed my arm in panic. She scream-
whispered, "He's coming this way." I turned quickly around and was
face-to-face with Kime. My face immediately flushed beet red, and I
started sweating profusely.

Kime, with casual Senior-type flair, said to me, "Your lips are chapped
and it's really gross." He then sauntered off into the crowd. In the
moment, I was not angry or embarrassed. I felt so relieved that I did not
have to respond. I had nothing clever to say.

My private revenge came later that day. I wrote a poem in math class to
document my feelings about Kime's betrayal.

a dead worm
pulled away
from the earth
to play in the rain
I turned to you
only to inhale
your rank stench
my lips cracked
and bled

I taped the poem to the inside of my locker for the remainder of the school year. Erin and I could recite it by heart. Our imaginary soap opera starring Kime and K-nic continued until they graduated in June.

49

A particular exchange I had with my dad when I was teen has always stuck with me.

One Saturday morning, before Dad left for the office, he told me to clean the garage. I worked from morning until lunch, making sure the garage looked spotless and orderly. When Dad got home, he said, "Well, let's take a look at how you did on the garage." Dad surveyed the garage, his eyes moving from corner to corner, finally resting on a sizeable pile of long boards. "Colleen," he said, "move one of those boards." I walked over to the pile of heavy boards and moved one. Underneath the board was some dirt. I had not thought to clean under the neatly stacked boards. Dad said in a calm, penetrating voice, "Colleen, if you're going to do something, don't do it half-assed."

I felt my failure. Dad went to dinner. I stayed and dragged the boards out of the garage and swept under them. Weirdly, though the moment also felt wonderful. I was guiltily thrilled. "Half-assed." My Dad used adult language with me. The first and only time. In my head, at that moment, I became an adult. Maybe a half-assed adult, but still an adult.

Dad would probably dislike that this is the memory that stays close in my mind and heart. He'd prefer I remember the time we went to the National Honor Society induction dinner. Grades. He trusted them.

50

When we were growing up, Jennifer and I followed the rules and accepted the plans set by our parents. Jane, not so much.

Jane was not a bad child by any stretch, just hard-wired for independent thinking. First, there was the Underwear Rebellion of 1969. When Mom did laundry, she put all the girls' underwear in one deep dresser drawer. Predictably called "the underwear drawer." We three girls shared one drawer of clean underwear. About age seven, Jane balked. She flat out told Mom that she did not want to share the same underwear with Jennifer or me. Mom took Jane aside to have a talk. Jennifer and I were not sure what they discussed, but from that point on Jane had her own private drawer filled with Jane underwear. Jennifer and I continued to pick from the communal drawer.

And there was the Landscaping Compromise of 1976. During the summer months, Dad decided that his four children would work on the yard all day, every Saturday. For the entire summer. New house. Much to be done. The first Saturday, we dug drainage trenches, hauled wheelbarrow loads of pebbles, and, to break up the monotony, unearthed saplings in the adjacent woods and transplanted them in our yard. The next Saturday mountains of black dirt and mulch sat in the driveway ready to be moved. As Dad was giving instructions on the day's work ahead, Jennifer interrupted, "Where's Jane?" Dad explained that Jane proposed that she clean the house instead of working outdoors. Dad said the arrangement made sense: beautiful yard and clean home. Jane again thwarted the mandated paradigm.

And then, the legendary College Plot of 1979. Jane was scheduled to graduate high school in 1980. Jane, however, told my parents that she didn't want to finish high school. She wanted to go directly to college after finishing 11th grade. Jane, of course, had a plan. She took her SAT test. Scored well. She researched colleges. Applied to a college that did not require a high school diploma. Jane only needed a qualifying SAT score. In the Fall of 1979, Jane went off to college. Her plan did not stop there. Jane earned straight A's her first year of college. And although University of Michigan did not accept high school students without a GED, the school did accept college transfer students. Jane transferred to the University of Michigan in the Fall of 1980. Jane prevailed. Again.

51

I loved one movie in high school. Only a 57% on the Rotten Tomato-meter. *Vision Quest*, a coming-of-age movie about Louden Swain, a high school wrestler. Louden plans to drop weight classes, so he can wrestle the local legend, a wrestler named Shute. Going a full six minutes on the mat with Shute is Louden's vision quest. Louden's coach warns him, "No one wants to fight Shute."

My high school vision quest was not Louden Swain noble: I wanted a boyfriend. I was not sure how to make a boyfriend happen. No experience. An opportunity soon presented itself. I had a babysitting job three doors down from my house. The child went to sleep early. I telephoned Jim who used to live near me—a newspaper delivery and lawn service connection. I told him I was babysitting and asked if he wanted to come over and play Yahtzee. He did. We played. When the game ended, we kissed. A little. Not a lot.

The next week Jim came to watch me play basketball. Coach Holmes put me in the game because we were stomping the other team. My parents never came to see me play basketball. Jim did. Now, Jim knew: I was bad. An athletic disaster. Jim didn't care. I broke up with Jim a few days later, not that we were a couple. Or anything. He was wearing a soft cotton fisherman's sweater. The sweater felt right. The feelings were too strong. For me.

Later that winter, Jim and I went to the Detroit Zoo together. Still friends. It was cold. I loved that day. Chaste. But intimate. Jim would later tell me that the zoo trip was a defining moment in his life. His words: "Never have I been more in love. Never more at ease with a person. And contrary to my original teenage lust, it taught me that love is more than conquest."

52

I had my own car. A hand-me-down yellow Nova. Plaid seats. I now felt as if I could control my life, driving to and away from whatever I wished. It was summertime. I called Tilda. I missed her.

"Tilda, do you want to come over my house for a sleepover?"

Tilda agreed. The next day I pulled into Tilda's circle drive. She was sitting on the porch waiting for me and quickly jumped into my car. For the next fifteen miles, we laughed and talked.

Tilda then bent over and pulled a cigarette out of her tote. But it wasn't a cigarette.

"Tilda, I cannot have drugs in my car."

"Calm down," Tilda said as she lit up.

I once again resorted to reciting the Our Father. Not out loud this time. Just in my head. If a police officer pulled me over, there were drugs in my car. I was freaking out. Internally. I turned the car around and took Tilda back to her house.

Sleepover canceled.

53

My first boyfriend in the traditional sense happened in 12th grade. On the first day of school, we reported to advisory. Advisories were populated according to last name, so I was with all the E students. A classmate whom I did not know sat down next to me. Sam.

Sam talked to me. An unusual occurrence. Boys did not flock to me. Later that week, Sam asked me out. We went out. We had two or three subsequent dates. Sam had recently broken up with his long-time girlfriend. Not a dating novice.

Sam was intelligent, kind, funny, and confident. Popular. He planned to be a dentist. Dad loved Sam—especially the dentist part. I liked Sam. He was out of my league. I was still so awkward being me that I was not capable of maintaining a romantic relationship, but I tried.

Sam asked me to the Homecoming Dance. I accepted. After a good time at the dance, he drove me home and I invited him into my house. We made out on the family room yellow plaid couch. I liked kissing, but then Sam tried to take off my pantyhose. Thankfully, Mom came downstairs, quelching the cliché teen moment. And my panic.

Blessed with late Fall summer temperatures, the next weekend Sam and I met friends—other couples—at a local beach. I was a couple. I was out of my element. Stuck with a group of age-mates. Hormonally charged. Lots of couple-touching. I was not without hormones, but my hormones were a private matter.

A game of volleyball was played. Everyone played. I wasn't good but I did participate. Much better than small talk or public displays of affection. The day was hot, so many boys took off their shirts. Sam took his shirt off. The moment proved bigger than me. I could not handle the semi-nakedness of it all. Sam had a third nipple. An expected surprise.

And he was still fine. Completely comfortable. No teen angst.
I was a mess.

I was not ready for the physicality of dating. The public intimacy.
Coupledom. Too much. I broke up with Sam the next day.

54

I do not remember how I met Henry—only that he was funny and in my
English class. Well-liked. Smart, but considered a jock. Henry was an
exceptional athlete. He played basketball and golf at a high level.

Henry and I got along well together. No expectations, no bravado. I
could talk to Henry, but there was no official first date. Henry simply
and seamlessly became a welcome member of my household, and
he got along with my brother Chris. He even helped with Saturday
landscaping—winning my dad over. My guess is that Henry and I
were both not ready for adulthood. Both clueless how to manage the
transition from near adulthood to actual adulthood. The adhesive of our
eventual romance.

Henry wanted to be a professional golfer. I wanted to be a teacher. At
the end of the school year, Henry asked me to prom. We went. Henry
wore a brown tuxedo with an ascot. All the other boys wore bowties and
enviously eyed Henry's ascot. I wore a modest cream gown clumsily
managing the evening. A large social event, requiring much self-talk to
manage the event. All and all, I made it through.

Henry and I hung out during the summer. My parents were out of town
nearly all of it. Deregulation destroyed their Michigan business, so they
were in the process of opening a real estate company in Florida.

After I left for college in South Carolina, Henry still hung out at
the Michigan house with Chris. No parents around. They probably
have stories.

55

I spent about two hours getting ready, putting my hair up in barrettes;
then, down again. Finally, I decided to wear it up. I was going to see Jim
before I left for college. Jim was home on a break from the Air Force.
I drove over to Jim's house in my Nova. Jim was messing with things
under the hood of his truck. He stopped.

I wore a grey University of Michigan t-shirt. Jim was wearing his choker
necklace. He was tanned. Always dark. Olive-skinned. I was pale.
Always deathly pale. We talked in the driveway. It was the first and only
day I met Jim's mom. Jim played the meeting in cool-guy mode.
I deserved it.

Jim told me I looked like one of them. We talked of them as people who
went through life living and feeling without too much thinking. Both Jim
and I were overthinkers. Right before I left, Jim told me that I should not
wear my hair up. Down. Natural was better. He touched my hair.

I used to feel I was better for not being a them, but, in retrospect, I should
have spent more time actually living and feeling.

Jim remembers the college good-bye differently. His words:

"Okay, here's how that day replays in my mind. You show up—ethereal
in young auburn haired and sublime beauty. To say good-bye. You were
so clean and pure in my mind and eyes. I was busying myself so I would
not be making a fool of myself. I don't know what being one of them
meant to me. I know I felt I was going to be lost to you, and I remember

clearly what that meant to me. When I touched your hair (or was it your face) there were no clean or pure thoughts in my mind at all."

56

My parents were not in town when I left for college. Jane dropped me off at the Detroit Metropolitan Airport. I navigated check-in. The counter agent doubted my taped cardboard box of college supplies was sturdy enough. The flimsy box sat next to my Diane Von Furstenberg suitcase, a graduation gift from my parents.

I kept it emotionally together until I settled into my seat and was prompted to prepare for take-off. Tears started to fall. Understandable. I was leaving the familiar and heading toward the unknown. A priest was seated next to me. He questioned, "Why are you crying?"

"I am leaving home and going to college."

"Do you want to go to college?"

"Yes."

"Then, why are you crying?"

I cried harder. A good cry is a good cry—even if an inconvenient public spectacle. A private cry is preferred; but when tears come, they come. At least in my world. By the time the airport shuttle dropped me at campus, I was composed.

College was busy. Classes. Homework. Job. Jane, who was now attending University of Tennessee, came to visit me for a long weekend. She brought me two packages: an oversized twin comforter with tight stripes of pink, yellow, green, and blue along with a matching pink quilted pillow sham. Jane and I washed the bedding in the college laundry and then made up my dorm bed. Jane's gift cemented a life maxim: good bedding is love. I felt it.

57

My time in college is intertwined with my time in food service. Education came easily. Waitressing did not. Waitressing is no longer a standard term, but I was a waitress, not a server.

I was hired to open a brand-new sports bar. I had to pass a three-week training boot camp for the store opening. I aced the menu test. I aced food service. The beverage service hurdle was high. I knew nothing about beer, liquor, mixed drinks. When a practice customer asked, "Do you have Dos Equis?" In my head I said, "What?" Aloud I said, "Let me check for you, sir. I then ran to the bartender and said, "Do we have doohickeys?" Luckily, the bartender liked word puzzles. We muddled through my ignorance together. I graduated from training. When the training team was readying to leave town, the lead trainer came over to me and said, "You know, at every restaurant opening, at the start of training, we try to identify who is not going to make it. Not one of us thought you'd make it." My trainers had been quietly anticipating my failure. Big internal frown. But he smiled, seemingly glad I surprised them. He did not understand my motivation. Economic necessity.

I worked at the local taco place. The drive-thru line was crazy after football games. It was my first exposure to a fast-paced, time pressure situation—other than standardized testing. Drive-thru customers were rather grumpy when they had to come inside to fix a wrong order. I managed the proverbial heat of the kitchen, learning to rectify mistakes quickly and move on. No time for emotional wallowing. Additional lessons were given in exhaustion and conformity. And I had to wear a hairnet. No glamour.

I worked at a seafood restaurant chain. Diner-style. The all-you-can-eat fish fry and fried clam nights made the drive-thru bustle seem like the minor leagues, especially when the kitchen staff was unable to maintain a steady supply of fries, fish, and clams for waiting guests. Once, when I was waitressing at a lobster house, we ran out of lobsters. As a waitress, I was often on the edge of failure or smack on the frontline of failure.

Failure. Failure is a hard word to just let be. I am wary of the need to reframe failure as something other than or more than failure. Failure is failure. No need for repackaging. Failure does not have a heavy weight unless I give it a heavy weight.

If food service taught me anything, it is to approach failures—big and small—without qualification or aggrandizement, mitigate my emotional response and work to fix it.

58

At college, I was placed into a 2-person suite. The arrangement did not last long. My roommate wanted a friend. I did not have the capacity to be what she needed. I stopped talking to her. Shortly thereafter, she moved out. I was blissfully alone. I attended my classes, did my homework, lifted weights, rode a stationary bike, and ran around the track, and worked food service 20 hours a week.

I had two near-relationships with co-workers. Jeremy told me he was a member of the United States Olympic team—the year the United States boycotted the Olympics. He had pictures with the team but did not get to live his dream. Jeremy had incredible thighs. Muscular. He was older than me. Nice and hard-working. We went on a few dates. He introduced me to his parents. He invited me to his apartment. I volunteered to make dinner: Shake 'n Bake pork chops, canned Le Sueur peas, and Jiffy corn muffins. I was raised to be brand loyal. After the meal, Jeremy invited me to stay over. A chaste sleepover. No pressure. I had hidden a toothbrush in my purse. I brushed my teeth, and we went to bed. We kissed and

held each other. Jeremy was beyond me in age and maturity. Very calm.
I stopped seeing Jeremy after I returned to campus following Winter
Break—my relationship with Henry rekindled during my time at home.

Later in the Spring though, I played frisbee and went on a motorcycle
ride with Rico who was a drive-thru cashier, like me. Rico was from
New York. He was funny and worldly. He invited me over to his place.
He picked me up on his motorcycle, we stopped and snagged a half
gallon of fudge ripple ice cream, and we settled in to watch television at
his apartment. Two spoons—eating out of the ice cream carton. Rico and
I had little in common, but he could talk. Wonderfully so. He talked all
night. No sex. No pressure. A kiss or two. After the overnight, we kept up
our work friendship. I liked being around Rico.

59

I love the word *underbelly*. It is appropriately meaningful and sounds
edgy: "the soft underside or abdomen of an animal," "an area vulnerable
to attack," or "a hidden unpleasant or criminal part of society." I have
always trusted that every good place, even college, has an underbelly.
Every home has an underbelly. Vulnerabilities. Unpleasantness. But
because the underbelly is the *under*belly—it is a relatively small part of
the larger whole.

I have not always cozied up to the expression "every cloud has a silver
lining." Case in point. My sister Jane had a boyfriend at the time of
college graduation. Pete. She was young. He was young. They were
both a week away from earning their business degrees. In a spontaneous
moment, they went to the courthouse and were married. A week later,
they graduated. Another week later, they were both offered jobs—in
different states. Texas and Tennessee. A week later, they filed for an
amicable annulment. Pete left for Texas. Jane was heartbroken.
As Mom and I were helping Jane pack up her college apartment, Jane
began sobbing.

Mom turned to Jane and, in all seriousness, said gently, "Think about your diploma." Jane and I looked at each other and then laughed uncontrollably. Until Jane cried again. Mom's request to focus on a possible silver lining seemed so clueless. Ridiculous. To this day when something awful happens, Jane and I both say, "Think about your diploma." It's now oddly comforting. Still, I would argue that it is much easier to reconcile that a big, good thing has an underbelly than it is to accept that a big, bad thing has a silver lining.

60

After my first year at college, I came home to disarray. Family financial crisis. Full blown. The Michigan house was empty, except for Chris and me. My parents were still in Florida still attempting to recapture stability.

As my parents' world was imploding, I wasn't adequately prepared for the upheaval. I didn't know how to be alone in the awfulness. I didn't know how I was going to continue in college. After just one night back home, I reached the end of my emotional line. I made two phone calls. I first called Jim. He wasn't home and his mom said, "Is this Susan?" I hung up—feeling stupid. Why would he be there for me? I took a deep breath. My second call was to Henry. He was home. I was relieved.

Henry bought a Gran Torino, the passenger-side riddled with bullets, and volunteered to drive Chris and me to Florida. We loved the car. His mother wept as we pulled away. Henry was the youngest of five. The baby of the family. We made it to Florida, although we did have a flat tire in Ohio. Chris, Henry, and I moved into my parents' three-bedroom condominium, a remaining asset. The condominium association disapproved of the Gran Torino parked in the onsite parking lot. I took a waitressing job at a diner; Henry took a job at a national pizza chain—on the fast-track to becoming a store manager.

At some point, Henry and I went to see *Conan the Barbarian*. The movie awakened my hormones—dreaming of Conan, content to be with Henry.

A week later, I proposed to Henry. We married at the county courthouse. The county judge said to Henry, "Take care of her."

61

A few months after saying "I do," I was working a shift at the diner when I realized that I hadn't had my period that month. I went home and took a pregnancy test. Positive. Half of me thought, "Knocked up at nineteen." The other half of me giddily thought, "I am going to have a baby." I ate a Salisbury steak TV dinner that night—hoping to give the baby all the nutrients needed.

62

"Jane, it's going to be okay. Think of something positive." Jane usually consoled me. I looked to her to coach me through life. Tables turned. She had just broken up with a boyfriend. I sat in the passenger seat of Jane's Volkswagen Rabbit. The Rabbit was an odd color. Buffish. Almost ecru. Jane's tears continued. She finally allowed herself to breathe.

"I do have my car," she said in shift toward positive thinking.

"That is huge." I said as we sat at a red light.

"The only thing I have is my car." Her lips quivered slightly. Jane hiccupped another deep breath and proceeded to go through the green light.

In that moment, a sports car going full speed ran the red light, hitting Jane's car about two feet above the passenger door. Jane and I screamed. The driver of the other car came over. I rolled down my window. He yelled at us, "I needed to hit something." It looked to me like the accident filled him with additional rage. He paced frantically, muttering profanity.

"Jane, are you okay?"

"Physically. Yes. Now, I have nothing."

"There is a gas station a little way up the road. Do you think you could walk there for help? My door is crushed in."

"I am too upset." And she was. I was, too.

Two police cruisers arrived before we had to walk anywhere. One cruiser managed the scene, directing traffic and securing tow trucks for the vehicles. The other managed us. As an officer questioned Jane and the driver, a second officer used a handheld Jaws of Law extractor to wrench open the passenger-side door. I was free. He helped me stand up—sore, awkward, and wobbly. Nine months pregnant. I noted the driver of the sports car was handcuffed and loaded into their cruiser. A third cruiser pulled up and gave Jane and me a ride home. That officer said to me, "You should go to the emergency room to get checked out."

63

The emergency room doctor ran through a litany of questions. Only one question caused me embarrassment.

"What did you have for breakfast?"

"Cereal." Asked and answered. But the doctor probed.

"What kind of cereal?" It took me a second or two to respond.

"Coco Puffs." Deep humiliation uttering those two words. The doctor just kept up with more questions. He decided that it was wise to induce labor. Why take a risk with the accident and all? I was already two days past my due date. They put me in a labor room. My obstetrician arrived and proceeded to use what felt like his entire arm to break my water. Contractions began.

I used the clock to help me keep my composure during contractions. I made a deal with myself: When I felt the onset of a contraction, I would allow myself to scream if and when the secondhand circled the clock one full rotation. I spent a full minute concentrating on the secondhand rather than focusing on the pain. I never had to scream. The baby born without much discomfort or drama. The doctor and nurses gave me high praise. Holding my new baby, I felt a deep, deep love. I also felt terror, "What have I done?" I had no clue how to be a parent. Not even the basics.

Henry said, "If you let me name this baby, you can name the next." I agreed. Generosity abounds when a healthy baby is born. Sarah was named Sarah, meaning princess. Her middle name, Christina, after my brother Chris.

Two days later, Jane met me at the mall food court. Jane had found her center again. I was relieved. She updated me on her car situation, "The Rabbit is being fixed. No cost. The other driver was at fault and had priors." Then she noticed I was trying to give Sarah regular milk in her bottle. Jane kindly chided, "Colleen, I think babies take formula, not milk."

"I ran out of what the hospital gave me."

First, Jane bought me some post-pregnancy jeans. Next, she stopped at the grocery store to pick up baby formula.

64

My parents gave me a career. Not a job, according to them. A career.
A pre-license real estate course was the first step. Then, the state exam.
I completed both. I passed. My parents explained that real estate was
a perfect career for a new mother. Real estate was a little too money-
forward for my liking. And too people-forward. But my parents had a
business, and I needed a career. Jane worked in the office, too.

At this point in time, the real estate office was a large trailer. On a
beautiful lot. The future office building was a work in progress. After I
was licensed, I spent my time as a real estate receptionist. I greeted the
walk-in traffic. Anyone walking in who was not deemed a serious buyer
was mine. I also prepared mailings to solicit listings. Cold calling by
mail. I surprisingly secured a few listings.

A septuagenarian property owner who was a local resident, renowned for
his property holdings, dropped into the office after receiving my listing
request in his mailbox. Following a short discussion, he suggested we go
for a drive to see his property. He insisted that we drive in his convertible
Mercedes. I did not argue. I did not have a car. The drive was scenic, but
it seemed to me that we drove directly to his house. No properties were
visited. He explained that he needed to run in to get something. Would I
like to join him?

"No, I'll wait in the car." I waited for a long time. He eventually came
out and drove me straight back to the office. I was confused. Jane
explained that he wanted a quid pro quo listing. A favor for a favor.

I said, "No way. That is so gross."

65

Once Dad and Mom left Jane and me alone in the office trailer. A short errand to run. In the winter, the trailer was cold. Dad was worried about the wall heaters getting too hot, so he kept the temperature setting ridiculously low. As soon as Dad and Mom left, Jane and I jacked up the heater settings. We luxuriated in the radiant warmth. But only for a few moments. I accidentally rolled my upholstered chair against the metal surrounding the heater. The chair burst into flames. Jane yelled, "Fire!" I dove to safety.

Jane screamed, "Put it out! Dad and Mom will be back any minute!" I doused the chair with water from the water cooler. Jane said, "We need to hide the chair." We dragged the chair out of the trailer and threw it in the construction dumpster next to the parking lot. We went back inside the trailer. Wiped up the water. Sprayed the bathroom Lysol spray around the entire trailer. Opened the windows. Moved a backroom chair out front to replace the missing chair. Shut the windows. Turned down the heat. The trailer always smelled funky. Now, it smelled singed funky. Jane spotted our parents' car coming down the road. She shouted, "Look busy!"

Jane and I both ran to our backroom cubicles and pretended to be immersed in work. Dad and Mom came in. They were working on something big, so the new smell in the trailer was not a priority. Perhaps not even noticed. Dad did check on us later.

Jane told him she had an appointment to show a shopping plaza that afternoon. Dad said, "Good work." When Jane went to show the plaza, she did not return to the trailer. The person she showed the property to was her future husband, Frank. That first showing turned into their first date. My Dad was okay with that as long as Frank remained a sales prospect.

66

Henry and I had a second child two and a half years later. Planned. My obstetrician told me that I was carrying a boy.

When I was about eight months along, I started to get nervous, overthinking all the things that could go wrong. I made a direct appeal to God, "If you give me a healthy baby, I will never have another child." When I went into labor four weeks later, I walked from our apartment to the nearest payphone to tell Henry it was time to go to the hospital.

A healthy girl was born. I planned to name her Sophie Elizabeth. Jennifer, however, gave me a lecture over the hospital phone: "Colleen, what if Sophie becomes a professional. Give her a professional name. Sophia, not Sophie." So I did, Sophia Elizabeth. But I called her Sophie—unless we were in a professional setting. Sophia means "wisdom."

Baby Sophie had facial hair, thick red fuzz across both sides of her face. Startling. The nurses reassured me that this was normal; the face fuzz would fall off soon. Thinking I was having a boy, I brought a sailor's outfit to the hospital, so Sophie wore it home. She did not mind. I was tired and happy. Five days after Sophie was born, we moved to another city. Henry had been promoted to a higher volume store.

Sophie was an easy baby. Quiet, inquisitive, loved to nap. At just a few months old, Sophie attended her first wedding. I was a bridesmaid at Jane's wedding to Frank. Jane made Jennifer and I wear magenta bridesmaid's dresses with a massive floral pattern. Huge puffy, ruched sleeves. I was just a few months post-pregnancy, so my belly stretched the flowers into odd shapes. Jennifer and I were pretty sure Jane was trying to make us look curtain-hideous, so she would look prettier by contrast. Jane was breathtakingly beautiful on her wedding day. Sophie never made a loud sound the entire ceremony and reception—only coos and smiles. Jennifer fell in love with her and offered to take her.

67

Henry and I were lucky to have two intelligent, strong daughters. Henry acted as the primary provider for the family. He mistakenly handed me his paycheck each week, something his father did. His mother could have taught a master class on saving money. I could not.

68

When teaching 2-year-old Sarah the alphabet, I was proudly aggressive. My ABC flashcard drills included a lightening round during which Sarah sometimes cried.

I signed Sophie up for soccer at age 5. At her first game, I was confused when I watched her run. Her arms swung, dangled, and flopped at her sides. Her arms were flailing all over the place. Panicked, I turned to Henry, "Why is she not bending her arms? Why is she just letting her arms hang there like that?"

Over the next week, with boot-camp extremism, I explained to Sophie that she should hold her arms at a 90-degree angle when running. She endured a week of running drills with me barking, "Where are your arms? Do you know where your arms are? Get them up!"

I was my dad. Type A. Maybe Type A+. And then some.

69

Sarah, Sophie, and I had a road trip rule: Junk food is allowed. Apple Jacks cereal replaced oatmeal and blueberries. If the girls started making too much noise in the back seat. I threw back a bag of Cheetos to quiet them. No judgement, no lectures.

Once, we pulled into fast food place. Young me ate fast food (and Cheetos). What unfolded at the fast-food place was not pretty. I had, in front of my young daughters, an emotional moment. A meltdown. I was road weary.

The girls and I went inside to order, dutifully stretching our legs. The line was lengthy but moved quickly. Soon we were front and center at the aluminum counter. I ordered one chicken nugget kid's meal with a Barbie toy for Sarah, one plain hamburger kid's meal with a Matchbox car for Sophie, and one double cheeseburger for me.

"I am sorry. We don't have a double cheeseburger on the menu," the cashier replied. I took a moment to process this information. A moment in a fast-food restaurant feels like an eternity. The cashier waited for me to amend my order, maintaining eye contact and looking as if a prompt response was expected. I returned his stare, but I felt a twinge inside, an internal shifting.

"I always get a double cheeseburger," I said in reply to the cashier.

"We do not have double cheeseburgers at this location," he chirped. The chirp sounded inappropriately pleasant. Bad news should be delivered in a somber tone.

"Do you have a cheeseburger?" I asked, still calm but on the brink of something bigger.

"Yes," he said.

With a nearly undetectable quiver in my voice, I asked, "Can I order two cheeseburgers and have them put together to make a double cheeseburger? You, know, a special order." My strategy: Mix things up with straight-line logic and a customer-is-always-right hopefulness.

"No, ma'am. We do not have double cheeseburgers."

I almost managed dignity. But the dam broke. Road tears began streaming down my face. I loudly, too loudly, way too loudly, surrendered: "Just give me two cheeseburgers and I will put them together myself!"

My daughters in their Cheetos-stained T-shirts stared at me. Mortified. The lengthy line of customers looked away. Thankfully the serve time was brief. The girls and I were able to make a quick getaway. When safely back in the car, I collected myself, I gave the girls their kids' meals, I assembled my double cheeseburger from two single cheeseburgers and pulled away.

As we merged back onto the highway, I announced to the girls a new road trip rule: Every traveler is allowed one emotional breakdown each road trip. No judgement, no lectures.

70

Mom became a respected, successful real estate broker. Steeped in amortization tables, PMI, closing costs, depreciation, taxes. Logical and predictable. For a brief stint, however, she dabbled in Beanie Baby economics. Her collection grew to sixty Beanie Babies. Flash the Dolphin. Patti the Platypus. Squealer the Pig. Chocolate the Moose. And so on. I was embarrassed by Mom's Beanie Baby side-hustle, albeit thankfully and literally a closeted hustle. The amassing of plush toys seemed so out of character. Irrational.

Mom, for better or worse, had a favorite Beanie Baby. Does one disclose this about one's mother? Posthumously. Yes. The Princess Diana Beanie Baby—a deep lavender bear with a white rose on the chest and a purple ribbon bowed around the neck. Mom, whose maiden name was O'Neill, on occasion spoke of her English ancestry with pride and a proper air. She was deeply saddened by the untimely death of Princess Diana. The evening of the tragedy, Mom wrote a poem. Poetry writing, like Beanie

Baby collecting, was not in keeping with Mom's exterior persona. Not the person we knew.

Princess Diana
Not just another pretty face
Who pleases us and passes on.
Hearts are broken
That she's gone.
Time, whose course relentless runs,
Grant quick solace to her sons.
We will deal with
This fate's quirk,
And weave her star
Into our work.

Mom's zeal for Beanie Babies eventually waned. She gifted her cache of Beanie Babies to my sister Jennifer, who, at the time, had two young sons. Although the boys are now adults, the Beanie Babies are still around. They are in a rustic, large-sized basket in Jennifer's cabin. A generation of children have delighted in the toys and now a second generation. No market value. But thought priceless.

71

Sarah was an it-takes-a-village child. Her athletic coaches and academic teachers worked with me to raise Sarah, kindergarten to 12th grade.
All hands-on deck.

Once I took Sarah and Sophie to a city park—just down the road from the house we were renting. Sarah had just received a new pair of roller blades for her birthday and was calmly and contentedly rolling back and forth on the sidewalk. Sophie asked me to take her to the swings. A short hike from the sidewalk. Sarah begged to stay where she was— contentedly rolling. Okay—Sophie and I would return soon. While I was pushing the swing and talking to Sophie, I would periodically look over my shoulder to check on Sarah. All good.

Eventually I became preoccupied with Sophie and forgot to look over at Sarah. And Sarah was a child who needed watching. When I finally did look back over toward the sidewalk, there was a crowd of parents gathered. I heard more than one adult ask, "Where is her mother?" I grabbed Sophie and ran toward the mob.

As I neared, I could hear Sarah howling in pain and screeching, "Get away from me! Don't touch me! I want my mom!" The parent-crowd parted to reveal Sarah sprawled out on the sidewalk. Her right arm bent in an impossible direction or two. Even while in obvious pain, Sarah was trying to kick anyone who tried to help her.

With feigned dignity and calm, I pulled Sarah to her feet, threw my jacket over her arm, and said, "Sarah, don't look at it." I kissed her forehead and carefully carried her to the car, dragging Sophie with my free hand. At the hospital, Sarah was casted up. I thought the worst was over.

It wasn't. Cast removal time arrived. When I took Sarah to the doctor to get the cast removed, I did not anticipate the drama. I should have. I didn't. When the nurse and doctor tried to saw the cast off, Sarah screamed and fought back. She was uncontrollable. The doctor told me I would need to reschedule Sarah for another time. Sarah's strength and determination were uncommon. The adults needed to regroup.

Henry managed the second appointment. He put a coat over Sarah's head and held her down as she wailed and struggled. A doctor and two nurses triple-teamed Sarah and were able to remove the cast.

I am wired for self-control. No histrionics. Rarely wild abandon. I am a bit jealous of and fascinated by Sarah's emotional range. There is beauty in it. Sarah is the only daughter who has screamed, "I hate you!" in my face. I was upset at the time but also marveled at how liberating such an outburst might feel.

72

Real estate was not my calling. Henry and I eventually moved back to Michigan to live with his parents, so I could complete college. Henry's mother generously offered to watch Sarah and Sophie when I went to classes. Henry's mom was enormously good to me, Sarah, and Sophie. As was Henry's dad. They changed my life.

I was able to afford college, because I received a Returning Mother's Scholarship funded by a local community group. The recipient had to have at least one child and been out of college for a minimum of two years. I qualified. The scholarship did not cover all costs, but I paid the remaining balance by waiting tables.

I went through an Isaac Asimov phase during my college years. Asimov wrote a short story titled "The Immortal Bard." The story is about a character named William Shakespeare who is transported from the 1600s to the 20th century and enrolled in a college class on Shakespeare's plays. Spoiler alert. Shakespeare flunks the Shakespeare class. Asimov claimed he wrote the story as a revenge piece on English teachers—saying he, too, would probably flunk a class on his own writings. Asimov's story gave me solace when I felt in over my head in college. I could think, "Even Shakespeare would have flunked this. And maybe Asimov, too."

Overall, I loved college. A highlight of my first semester was a comment on an English paper. Professor Grimm wrote, "This sentence is particularly fine." I smiled for weeks. I earned a Bachelor of Arts in English and then applied to be an English Department graduate assistant. I had to interview for the position. My first high stakes interview. I was asked to describe how I was different from other candidates. This was a softball question given my parents' financial struggles and my teen pregnancy. I was awarded the position.

As a graduate assistant, my master's program tuition was paid, and I received a small stipend, an annual $1000, if I remember correctly.

The two-year program flew by. In my last semester, I was required to deliver a lecture to a group of undergraduate students while two associate professors watched and evaluated me.

My voice shook with anxiety as I tried to tell the class what I knew about Milton's *Paradise Lost*. My nerves and self-consciousness were on full display for three hours. A night class. While I lectured, I mentally chastised my former elementary school, middle school, and high school teachers for not pushing me to tackle public speaking, never making me step outside my shy nerd comfort bubble. But, in all honesty, I owned that moment. I hung back all those years. Not ready.

The lecture felt horrible, and I never wanted to see anyone who was in that room ever again—too embarrassing—but it was a huge hurdle jumped over. I survived talking in front of others. Surviving an experience is sometimes the point. Not accolades.

And I had a master's degree. Next, I needed a teaching job.

73

My sister Jane has been married more than once. A family pattern. All four of us—Jennifer, Jane, Chris, and I—have had at least two marriages.

Jane's second husband Frank drove into our lives in a Toyota Celica with sheepskin seat covers. Purchased used. Prudently so. Eventually replaced with a child-friendly vehicle. A Volvo Station Wagon. Purchased used. Prudently so. In sum, Frank and Jane had three children. All very, very wonderful. Frank, born and raised in Florida, is a Horatio Alger of sorts: a combination of genetic genius and colloquial cunning.

At the point Frank entered my life, he operated a waterbed business. A boots-on-the-ground approach: selling, delivering, assembling waterbeds. Eventually two storefronts. He referred to himself as "The Waterbed

King of North Florida." At some point, Frank transitioned to life as a commercial landlord. A big part of Frank's success was his frugal nature—weighing every purchase and meticulously reviewing every receipt, invoice, contract. Sensible. Shrewd. Wicked smart. Crazily so.

Mom and Dad never talked to Jennifer, Jane, Chris or me about money when we were growing up. Our childhood was an undulating socio-economic ride: rags to riches to rags to riches and so on. Salvation Army clothes in elementary and junior high. An aqua Cadillac and Florida condominium in high school. A financial crash. Mild peaks and valleys thereafter. Finances never discussed. Never. Unspoken mandate: No talking about money.

Their 1980s financial woes were not self-inflicted; deregulation imploded their business model. They were also navigating the world of money as rookies. They lived through the economic turbulence, including a stint living out of the car. Ultimately, Frank helped my parents settle a debt, allowing them to move forward. Unencumbered. Frank said my parents paid him back quickly—within a week. They achieved solvency and success again. No more dramatic fluctuations.

Frank saved me once also. While attending college, I waited on tables to pay for each semester. I was able to pay off the current semester just in time for the next semester. Except once. I was $780 short. Frank loaned me the $780 dollars. I finished college. A miracle of sorts. I eventually paid Frank back. I sometimes wonder if Frank didn't ask himself more than once, "What have I gotten myself into?" He married Jane. Not me or my parents.

Jane loved Frank. He loved her. Once we took a three-family vacation together—Jennifer's family, Jane's family, and my family. We stayed at The Roundhouse in Petosky, Michigan. Jane called our lodging the Rundhaus, drawing on her high school German. Jennifer and Jane paid my share of the vacation expenses. I had positioned myself as the charity case of the family: two children, paycheck-to-paycheck living, recent college graduate.

One evening at the Roundhouse, we played a game of Scrabble: Jane, Jennifer, Frank, and I. Frank preferred backgammon, but he was humoring us. The game was tight—until Frank played laid down the word R-E-N-A-I-L-E-R, exhausting his tiles and achieving point dominance. Jennifer and I vocally contested the prefix-suffix-dependent play. Jane looked at Frank adoringly and said, "Of course it is a word."

After a brief but vocal protest, Jennifer and I relented, because Frank is Frank and Jane is Jane. We were not going to win the argument. Frank is a brother-in-law legend in my mind, even with his illegal Scrabble win. Okay, maybe because of it.

74

My friend Rafael and I used to play a grouping game in college. We shared a few classes including Introduction to Psychology, a 3-hour night class. After a lecture on the Gestalt laws of grouping, Rafael and I decided to play a grouping game during the class break. One of us said a number and a topic; then, the other had to create groups—sometimes interesting, sometimes not but often our responses led to interesting conversation.

Rafael said, "Five. Beach."

I replied, "There are five groups of beach-goers: those who play in the surf at a reasonable distance from shore, those who swim out too far causing reasonable beachgoers worry, those who prefer an ankles-only water experience, those who build drip sandcastles, and those who insist on going to the beach but are annoyed by sand."

Digression. There is a sixth group: Those who purchase a townhome situated on the Gulf of Mexico, live in said townhome for seven years, and never once go to the beach. My parents. I asked Mom, "Why live on the beach if you are never going to go to the beach."

Mom replied, "Farris and I like the sound of the waves." Sound reasoning. No pun intended.

My turn. "Four. Cleaning."

Rafael replied, "I am going to do levels, not groups. There are four levels of household cleanliness: Level 1, an unclean household—visual mold or mildew and many piles; Level 2, a surface clean household with hidden piles; Level 3, a routinely clean household where everything has a place and is mostly in that place; Level 4, a perpetually clean household where everything has a fixed place within a place, color-coded. Three. Shopping."

"There are three groups of people: Those who faithfully redeem their Kohl's cash by the expiration date, those whose Kohl's cash is forgotten in the glove box, and those who are scratching their heads thinking, 'What is Kohl's cash?' Two. Food."

"Easy. There are two groups: Those who love cilantro and those who hate cilantro."

75

I love my daughter Sarah. To the moon and back. We are imperfectly matched. A person is not a single act or moment, especially a family member. But. When Sarah was young, we were at Cedar Point, an amusement park in Sandusky, Ohio, arguably the best in the world. Eighteen rollercoasters to date. Number 18—Steel Vengeance—opened May 2018. I should mention I like my two feet on the ground. Boats, planes, trampolines, and rollercoasters. Pass.

For those we love, we do things. The Gemini was touted as the "tallest, fastest, steepest" rollercoaster. Sarah and I stood in line. We were loaded into a seat. Steel bar firmly secured over our laps. The train of cars pulled away from the loading platform. After a few jarring turns and gentle hills, we began our ascent, slowly climbing to an apex of 118 feet. The climb was disturbingly slow, accented by the jerks and the sounds of scraping—in my mind—tired steel, seemingly on the edge of mechanical failure. Ka-chink. Pause. Lurch forward. Ka-chink. Pause. Lurch forward. Ka-chink. Pause. Lurch forward. Horrible. My heart was racing. I was saying the ABCs, over and over, in my head to stay calm. I was barely managing the moment. As we neared the top, just inches away from the 60 MPH drop and my imagined death, Sarah turned to me with an excited smile and said, "What are we going to do next?"

After surviving the ride, I went into full-on lecture-mode with Sarah. "Are you kidding me, Sarah? You need to live in the moment. You were done with the rollercoaster before it even finished." Luckily Sarah defied my rookie parenting. My absolutism. I wasn't wrong, but I wasn't right either. Sarah. Ever future-leaning.

76

After graduating from college, I immediately took the first job offered. A teaching position for the coming school year was not guaranteed. A furniture company specializing in sofa beds opened several locations in the Detroit area. I started as a sales associate at a convenient location, making a small salary per year plus commission.

I had to complete a two-week training program before I could hit the sales floor. I was taught to caress the sofa while introducing myself to customers and to sit down on the sofa when describing its features to potential buyers. I rehearsed how to gracefully become one with the couch until I could settle into the cushions with a compelling, casual ease. My fellow trainees and I suppressed giggles as we were evaluated on how well we lovingly and convincingly ran our hands across upholstery. We were rookies. We doubted that fondling an accent pillow had persuasive power.

I became a believer. I had a natural affinity for sofa sales, wired competitive and hungry for each commission. I delighted in the challenge of making a sale and tested each tenet of the training program. I was the top salesperson in the store for the month of July, my first full month after training. I fell in love with marketing and sales.

My stint in furniture sales did not last. In August, I landed a job teaching high school English.

77

My first teaching job was 9th grade English and Pre-Algebra. A package deal. Yikes. English, okay. I could manage even as a first-time teacher, because I had a relatively large pool of college English experience and much literature read. Pre-Algebra was a stretch. I knew I could stay a chapter or two ahead of students, but that is not the same as being an expert. Requisite depth lacking. The Pre-Algebra class was a temporary assignment until a qualified math teacher was found. I took it on. Temporary. Deep breath.

On my very first day of Pre-Algebra class a student raised his hand and asked, "Is zillion a real number?" I had no clue, but I was quick on my feet, albeit the question made me sweat. And I felt crummy inside.

"Zillion is a theoretical construct like all math," I replied and quickly continued with the lesson. That night, I went home and studied up on zillion. It was a pre-Google world, so the dictionary and other references helped me out. Zillion was not a number of any determinant value but referenced a large number in the general sense. I made sure to work that into my lecture the next day. Crisis averted.

As the job unfolded, I experienced teaching bumps. Not unexpected. Classroom management. No experience. I learned as disruptive behavior happened. Once a student walked into the classroom ten minutes late, munching a bag of chips. His demeanor was too casual. To me. "Please sit down and get your book out. And please put the food away. If you cannot get to class on time, you may not eat during class."

All was well for a few minutes. Then, I heard a crunch.

"Put the chips away." Another crunch. I lost it. "Pick up your books and chips and go to the office! You will never ever be in my classroom again!"

I ended up having to have a meeting with administration and the student the next morning. I apologized to the student for getting so angry. I explained that the chip moment felt so disrespectful. Yes, I could have handled it better. I did reaffirm that he needed to get to class on time. And if he did not get to class on time, he could not eat in class. I asked if he could manage that expectation. He agreed.

I had to get more creative and less triggered by what I deemed disrespectful behavior. I liked hokey teacher posters. One poster that graced the wall of my English classroom read "*Listen* and *silent* are spelled with the same letters." I loved the simple truth of the poster. If students were noisy, I would ask, "What is an anagram for listen?" They would respond, "Silent," in unison and settle down. A little magical. Once an independent-minded student responded, "Tinsel." I loved the intellectual push back.

78

A 6-foot-tall poster of William Shakespeare hung in my classroom. Paper William and I taught side-by-side for 16 years. When my students were noisy and unruly, I talked to Will as if he were alive: "William, can you hear me? I cannot hear myself in this noisy classroom." Students tend to quiet down when a teacher begins talking to a poster.

Grading was easier to master than classroom management. But there was still a learning curve. A student turned in a research paper draft on author Jack Kerouac. He misspelled Kerouac 32 times, 5 different variations: Keruac, Keruaec, Keraoac, Kearouac, Keraouc. Only a draft. No big deal. The series of the three vowels after the "r" in Kerouac is tough. And spelling has nothing to do with intelligence. I only expected polish and correct spelling on a final draft. On the student's rough draft I circled the misspellings in pencil, expecting them to be corrected on the final draft. A novice-level expectation perhaps.

Long story short or maybe short story long, the corrections did not happen. Misspellings remained on the final research paper draft. I circled each Kerouac spelling error in ink. My circles were excessive and emotional. And I used the word "insufferable" in my comments. A step too far. I was called into the principal's office for a meeting.

Kerouac probably would not have minded the student's misspellings. Even I now recall them fondly. There is a legend that Jack Kerouac typed his novel *On the Road* in three weeks on rolls of toilet paper taped together to form a continuous feed. His novel simply spilling out of him. But there was no toilet paper. It was a long scroll of paper—which still earns major cool points. The scroll draft was his first draft. There were many, many revisions. The scroll is in the American Writers Museum in Chicago.

As a teacher, I quickly realized that students had distinct developmental trajectories. Based on a zillion factors. Sometimes the developmental moment synced up with the class curriculum and sometimes it didn't. In time, I found asynchrony as beautiful as synchrony. I learned to approach expectations and grading with a high standard and nonjudgmental awareness. Lapses were part of learning. Part of growing up.

I also accepted that I was a flawed human. Owned my mistakes— sometimes tearfully so. I carried my learning forward. Shame was unnecessary but felt, nonetheless. Mostly, I kept my head down and worked hard. And learned. I loved teaching.

Above all, I learned that parents find a B+ the most infuriating grade.

79

Often the students in my classes had the kind of names picked for the protagonist of a bestselling novel or film: Amelia, Harrison, Gabriella, Arthur, Tahlia, Ross, Natalie, and Aliai. Remarkable names. Beautiful names. I even taught an Anakin. My name continued unremarkable. I never had a Colleen in my class. Ever.

80

In the lull of winter, I added a night job moonlighting as a Special Lecturer at my alma mater to supplement my teacher pay. I disliked the job title "Special Lecturer." Special was a bald euphemism for part-time and lecturer sounded reductive. My baggage. The job was life changing.

During my time at Oakland University, I taught business writing classes, mostly to business majors, routinely assigning student teams a multimedia presentation on a given topic at 6:00 p.m. to be delivered at 8:30 p.m.

I approached these evening classes as the academic equivalent of sofa bed sales training. I coached students how to write for a live audience and a reader. And to sometimes handle words like accent pillows. And sometimes like Scotchguard. To embrace and practice rhetorical strategy. I learned along with them. I was arguably invested way over-the-top, but the job felt like 11-years of play.

81

Sarah and Sophie were young when I started my first teaching job. At school, I found it incredibly easy to be patient with children who were not my own. I readily accepted that competency and excellence come with practice. Much practice. And much patience.

I realized that I treated my students better than my daughters. And my students were doing very well, academically and emotionally. I tried to make a subtle, but seismic correction. My daughters noticed. I was still Type A, but I embraced life with them differently. Whatever came.

82

I had to buy a gift for my grandmother-in-law. Henry's Mom's Mom. She was 97, opinionated and sharp-tongued. This was a gift-buying challenge. Family gatherings were still awkward, because I was an addition to the family. Not family proper. I decided to buy my new grandmother-in-law a kitschy, beautiful kitschy, Amaryllis-in-a Box. Basically, a potted flower bulb wrapped in cardboard box with the promise of an eventual bloom. I selected the Minerva variety with colors of a deep velvety red and a variegated white center. How could anyone dislike a flower?

On Christmas morning, my grandmother-in-law reigned in her much-complimented lilac-colored dress in her royal chair, surrounded by gifts. She opened her gifts one at a time. When she came to my gift, she tore off the big bow, ripped through the wrapping paper, and then opened the box. Upside down.

A big mess of potting soil fell into her lap. Grandma roared in anger and dismay, "Who gave me dirt?!!!" Silence. She became even more insistent, "I said, WHO gave me dirt?!" Silence. I was mortified and remained speechless.

83

Hot glue guns. The allure and facility of the tool are irresistible. Literally hot—and also harsh, but only if the user accidentally drips a drop of hot glue on his or her hand. Which always happens. A second of searing pain.

Cruelty expected and accepted.

84

My parents would eventually convince Henry and me to return to Florida to work at their real estate office. We moved back but only lasted a few months in real estate. Henry ended up returning to restaurant management. I found a teaching position. Henry continued to hand me his paycheck. I continued to be a disaster with money. We lived day-to-day. The years passed.

After moving to Florida. I immediately took an adjunct position teaching composition at the local community college. I graded many essays. Once I graded an essay with a startling opening line: "I woke up at the butt crack of dawn." Yikes. Butt. I did not allow Sarah or Sophie to say butt. I requested that they say bottom instead. I even told them I preferred the word ass over butt. Butt was a bridge too far. For me.

I circled the sentence and wrote, "Perhaps rethink your opening." I couldn't stop myself, I wrote more, "Does the usage of the word butt impact writer's ethos?" I continued to read the essay. The next couple of paragraphs were solid. Then, smack in the middle of the essay was one word, all-caps: "FUCK." I circled the word and placed three question marks nearby. The remainder of the essay was solid. I graded accordingly.

The next class, I returned the graded essays to students. The writer of the FUCK essay stayed after class to talk to me.

"Thank you for reading my essay," she said without embarrassment.

"You made a couple of interesting word choices."

"I apologize, but I have been putting that word in the middle of my essays as a test to know whether my professors actually read my work."

"I read it. What about your opening sentence?"

"'I woke up at the butt crack of dawn' is a regional expression. I do not think the word butt affects my ethos unless I have an out-of-area reader. You are an out-of-area reader."

"You are a good writer. I suggest avoiding butt and FUCK usage on your state writing exam, especially in all caps."

She smiled, "I will. Again, thank you for reading my essay and making comments."

I was offered a full-time position at the community college the next year, teaching composition, literature, and speech courses.

85

The next year, I taught a distance learning class. I had a regularly scheduled class with students on the main campus and two students way out at a satellite campus, 36 miles away. Joe and Trent. A new teaching challenge.

Each location was equipped with a large screen that broadcast the class in real time. More television-looking in style than monitor-looking. The camera followed sound so whoever was talking was front-and-center on display, student or teacher. Each location could see the other. A high-tech marvel at the time. The satellite students had an added gadget: a second camera that they could move at will to explore the classroom.

And they did. I had a secondary display on my desktop screen that allowed me to see what Joe and Trent were doing with that second camera. As I lectured or we discussed, Joe and Trent traveled the classroom with that second camera, taking close up looks at their main campus classmates. Despite their second camera wandering, Joe and Trent were dedicated students—prepared for class, participatory, interested, and interesting.

As the class unfolded, I noticed that the second camera settled more and more often on just one student. I drove out to the satellite campus to discuss second camera usage with Joe and Trent. A person-to-person meeting seemed wise. When I questioned them about the camera usage, Trent admitted that he had fallen in love. He used the word love. It was an awkward situation to navigate. More eHarmony than Composition 101. I called IT and had them remove the second camera for the remaining classes.

I invited Joe and Trent to attend the final class of the semester on the main campus, so they could meet their classmates in person. I brought doughnuts. Trent introduced himself to the student he had fallen for from his seat at the satellite campus.

86

I was driving over to pick up Sarah from the in-town high school. I saw her waiting on the curb. I kept driving. I headed to the county office complex. Just a few blocks farther. I went in and picked up a packet of do-it-yourself divorce papers. Papers picked up. I retrieved Sarah.

My marriage to Henry lasted seventeen years.

87

I was the party petitioning for divorce. Henry not to blame. We married young. Irreconcilable differences.

When I told Jennifer about the divorce, she said, "It's about time." Jennifer liked Henry, but she recognized our couple dysfunction. When I told my mom, she said, "Are you sure you know what you are doing?" Dad offered to pay for a lawyer. I told him that I would manage the divorce on my own.

Henry and I were mostly amicable through the divorce, but both of us hurt. We did not make accusations or fight. No badmouthing the other. That I know of.

Sarah and Sophie disliked me for a while, because I was the one who initiated divorce. I immersed myself in running and working—and researching divorce and its impact on children. One website offered a rough timeline: children experience two years of upheaval, followed by six healing years. I was reassured that the girls would be somewhat okay in two years and fully okay in eight years. It felt like a long road ahead.

After the divorce, Henry moved back to Michigan. Sarah, Sophie, and I moved in with my parents in Florida.

88

A framed poster hung in my dad's real estate office lobby. The poster pictured a gazelle and a lion. The wording on this poster summed up Dad's life philosophy:

"Every day in Africa a gazelle wakes up. It knows it must run faster than the fastest lion or it will be killed. Every morning a lion wakes up. It knows that it must outrun the slowest gazelle, or it will starve to death. It doesn't matter whether you're a lion or gazelle. When the sun comes up, you'd better be running."

Dad had a rocky home life, dropped out of high school, joined the Marines at 18, and, afterward, went on to own businesses. He prided himself on not working for anyone else. Dad never said "I love you" to me or my brother and sisters. That I know of. An uncle once whispered to me, "Your father is an asshole." Instead of feeling insulted, I felt proud. My dad—no argument—was difficult. Human relationships were not his forte. His expectations were high and messed up.

My dad saved me more than once, including taking Sarah, Sophie, and me in after my divorce. I repeatedly warned him, "Dad, this is temporary." He ignored me and asked the girls what colors they wanted their bedrooms painted. When the girls and I eventually moved out, my dad didn't talk to me or visit for a full year. He explained, "I just can't."

89

On my one-year my divorce anniversary, I ordered a refrigerator magnet online. A motivational mantra printed on it.

The words of poet Mizuta Masahide provided me steadfast resolve: "Barn's burnt down—now I can see the moon." Masahide's haiku described the upside of life crisis. My barn was burnt. I focused on the moon.

I emailed Jim three questions: What color work socks do you wear? What smell do you like to smell? Are you my weakness?

Jim's reply: "Brown. Wet dog. I wish."

90

A few weeks later, I emailed Jim again. I asked him to tell me a story. Jim grounded me.

His story:

"When I was eleven years old, I inherited the Detroit News paper route from my brother who no longer had time for it. My parents thought it would build character. I hated it. I was allergic to the newsprint. I hated the circulars that had to be inserted. I hated asking for money for services rendered. I made no money and, because I was miserable, it took me forever to complete the route every day. Then, the first winter came. The Sunday Edition was dropped at my house at 4:30 a.m. and was expected to be delivered by 6:00 a.m. At first, this seemed to me the worst hardship. Then, I started to look around those bitter cold winter Sunday mornings. There was no one else stirring within miles. Not a car passed (even on the main road). It felt as though I could have been the last person on Earth. Soon I found myself waiting for the papers to arrive. I had come to embrace that little bit of solitude. My home was a very hectic one. It was the first thing that ever felt like it belonged to me. To this day, I enjoy solitude. I have hiked the Grand Canyon alone. And Isle Royale. And Montana's Glacier Park. And when I hunt, I prefer to do it alone. I don't know if that was the character my parents had hoped to build all those years ago, but I learned to be comfortable with myself, and self-sufficiency for me is not a matter of survival but prosperity."

91

Dad was a less intense grandfather than he was a father. He took Sarah and Sophie on long road trips to explore graveyards, traveling as far as Nova Scotia. Banana splits instead of dinner was a thing. Homemade pie instead of dinner was a thing.

Dad was genealogy-obsessed. His surname, Elgee. He spent a good chunk of his nonworking hours trying to find a familial link to Irish poet and playwright Oscar Wilde whose mother's name was Jane Francesca Elgee.

Dad and Mom named my sister Jane Francesca Elgee—as if willing kinship. A definitive family link to Oscar Wilde was never found, but Dad was dogged in his hunt for one. Many, many years later, my dad received a posthumous gift: a great grandson named Oscar Farris.

92

I was able to secure a teaching job at my former school in Michigan— middle school English. And Sarah and Sophie were admitted. We would be moving back to the Midwest. I winnowed to our must-have possessions, keeping only what could fit in our Mercury Villager van. It was fully loaded. Near to the ceiling. The driver and passenger seat remained open. The second passenger had just enough room to lay flat atop our belongings in the rear of the van. I was joyous: We all fit.

Sarah, using anger and tears, secured the passenger seat. Sophie, who likely preferred to be separated from both of us during the family migration, relegated herself to the long narrow space above the packed goods. Before we were out of Alabama, Sophie convinced Sarah that her tight travel spot was superior to the spacious passenger seat ride, prompting Sarah to beg to trade places for the duration of travel. Sophie refused. She stayed cramped and miserable the remainder of the trip. Sarah's envy bringing her a measure of comfort.

It was a big summer for both girls. Sarah was ready to begin her final year of high school, returning to friends she knew. Still worried and stressed. Sophie was ready to begin high school, ninth grade. I do not know how she felt. Sophie cloaked her feelings. Sarah overshared; Sophie undershared. While the girls were not entirely keen about moving, they were glad to be moving near their dad. Close, accessible.

I arrived in Michigan a house-less, single mother. Jennifer took me in for a couple of months. More correctly, her family took me in. My brother-in-law Scott coached me to emotional equilibrium often, saying things like "It's just as easy to cry outdoors as it is indoors." He insisted the girls and I join in family adventures with him, Jennifer, and their boys. They were good to me. Beyond measure.

93

I found a two-bedroom loft apartment nearby. I could just swing things financially—sort of. I could pay rent, utilities, school tuition, and gas— food not so much. Luckily, a school parent asked me to tutor for $50 once a week on Wednesdays. Reading comprehension.

That Wednesday tutoring check became our weekly food allowance. It was embarrassing, but I cashed that check at the bank 15 minutes after receiving it. Every week. Next, the girls and I would visit the grocery store, attempting to spend wisely. Sophie argued for one blissfully good-tasting meal—no matter if we had to skip other meals. She dreamed of steak and real mashed potatoes. Instant potatoes were a common post-divorce starch. Sarah argued for consistent meals, even if bland. No meal skipping. We lived mainly on pasta and sauce, occasionally splurging on one good-tasting meal.

My tutoring gig was cancelled midyear. The family left the school.
About the same time, my dad forgave me for moving back to Michigan.
My mom started sending me $100 a month. From the time I gave
birth to Sarah at age 19, I created a life situation that I often could not
independently maintain. Guilt accompanied any support received, but it
is what I knew.

Expecting I might consider marrying again, Jennifer counseled me, "It is
just as easy to fall in love with someone with money than it is someone
without money."

I replied, "Jennifer, I have no money. You should be telling others not
to marry me."

I pushed money away from me. I worked hard, but I was money
avoidant. Books, tuition, and sports fees for the girls—funded without
thought. No savings. My acclimation to making poor financial decisions
was extreme. Once, when purchasing a used car at the dealership, I had
the choice between two white vans, each with 25,000 miles. Same price
tag. The only difference: one had a fog-like stain on the rear window, and
one didn't. I chose to drive away in the van with the stained window. I
am not going to psychologize it.

I started dating Jim. He was divorced with three daughters: Olivia,
Marne, and Corrine. He was frugal and blunt. He had been employed
since middle school. He was now in law enforcement. I was a teacher.
Seemed a good match.

94

I had a new mentor: Emery, the Middle School Director.

One of my most difficult colleagues was Emery. I mean difficult in the most respectful and beloved way. Emery was a mentor to me for 16 years—and his influence still impacts my approach to education.

Emery loved critical thinking. Even thinking about Emery made my brain hurt. With Emery, an idea was never just an idea but also its possible underpinnings and derivation which if left unconsidered lessened the quality of thinking. Emery had an endless patience when talking to students and colleagues always asking, "Why do you think this way?" He asked this question with an open mind, genuine curiosity, patience, and without judgement. Emery asked "Why do you think this way" even if he agreed with you. And he wouldn't tell you he agreed with you until you had completely articulated and self-vetted your own thought. Maddening. But healthy.

If Emery were to write a novel, somewhere in the plot, I am pretty sure a character would say, "You never really know your own mind until you question your own point of view…until you climb inside your brain and walk around in it." Emery helped me think, grow, and be. Happily so.

I also had a critic. An anti-mentor. A difficult colleague. Not good difficult. Any misstep or perceived misstep I made fed her. It hurt. I cried way too many times over public slights and backdoor insults. I knew I was not perfect. I made mistakes.

I hung an Eleanor Roosevelt quotation poster in my classroom: "Great minds discuss ideas, average minds discuss events, small minds discuss people." I learned to say hard things aloud. I realized that putting difficult topics and thoughts front and center was honest and good. I realized I was not going to be liked by all, especially by my anti-mentor. No chance. I stopped crying.

Once when feeling frustrated, I asked my colleague Bob how to get along better with human beings. I naively expected him to have a magic answer. Bob and I had a conversation. No real answers. A few days later, however, I got an envelope from Bob. It had the following quotation stuffed inside:

"Remember that the things others do that drive us crazy, are the very things that keep them functional."

I laughed. Felt relieved. I taped the quotation inside my office desk drawer. It reminded me to lighten up. And to remember that my perspective is not the only perspective.

95

For summer work, Sarah, Sophie, and I cleaned condominium rooms in Florida. My parents were in property management, so there was no shortage of rooms to clean. We were paid $50 a room. Our goal was four rooms a day; however, sometimes we were asked to do eight rooms. Summer was the height of season.

Sarah leaned into the teamwork, excelling at cleaning. Sophie balked at the job. She was capable but did not choose to clean. Instead, she provided running commentary as she surveyed each room's condition.

"What kind of people would leave a room like this?"

"Did you see the microwave? What did they put in there?"

Sophie kept Sarah and me laughing. We ended up assigning Sophie linen and towel collection and inventory. No cleaning. Again, a running commentary.

"Who would steal a washcloth?"

"Did you see the stain on these sheets?"

It was physical work. I loved the feeling of complete exhaustion after a day of cleaning. Sarah and Sophie did not share my enthusiasm, but they did like getting paid.

During the school year, I helped seniors with college application essays and future doctors with medical residency statements in an attempt to supplement my salary. I was good at working one-on-one, asking questions to pull together an essay or statement that was in their words and beautifully composed.

I was horrible at asking to be paid. I preferred working as a writing coach to cleaning, but I was not able to comfortably manage the financial side of it. If a client simply left a check in an envelope in my mailbox or on the table when leaving, great. But if they asked, "What do I owe you?"

I would mumble, "Nothing. We're good." Money was too personal to discuss.

Venmo didn't exist at the time. If it did, I could have just said, "Send me what you think is fair later." No face-to-face monetary exchange.

96

During my childhood, teachers were unbelievably good to me. I asked Jim which of his teachers had the most significant impact on him. His answer was immediate: Mr. Paul Barber, Music Director.

I cannot come up with a single person. To be honest, I remember bits and pieces of my teachers—physical attributes, snippets of shared time, leftover feelings. Miss Attaman, my 2nd grade teacher, wore a dress every day, had silky, long black hair, and never raised her voice. She was beautiful inside and outside. When Tilda and I played "school," we fought over who played Mrs. Attaman. We all wanted to be her.

My 6th grade teacher Mr. Slater had a beard. My 11-year-old self never knew an adult who had a beard, so I spent most of the school year watching his beard. He was single but married later in the school year. He liked baseball. He raised his voice sometimes. After Mr. Slater yelled, he spoiled us for the remainder of the day to make up for his outburst. Extra recess time. No homework. Bubble gum. Tilda—wise beyond her years—often pushed Mr. Slater to anger, anticipating the benefit of the kindness that followed.

Then there was my Catechism teacher Sister Kathleen. A classmate asked her why she had become a nun. Sister Kathleen shared that God asked her to be a nun. We asked, "How did he ask you?" She explained God came in her mind and asked her in her thoughts. I spent a good portion of that school year worried that God was going to come into my head and ask me to be a nun. I was sure if I said yes, I would be unhappy. I was sure if I said no, I was going to Hell. It ended up a false dilemma. The question never came.

Mrs. Siobel was my 9th grade Biology teacher who did not shave her legs, was genius-smart, and had little patience for giggling girls. She lived and loved science. We apprehensively sat for her exams. There were no bonus points. No corrections. But always the invitation to repeat the class. If my friends and I had still played "school" in high school, we would have fought over who got to be Mrs. Siobel.

Coach Holmes taught 11th grade history and ran grueling 3-hour Saturday morning basketball practices. I was not a standout player, but he pushed me anyway. With Coach Holmes, life was simple. Know the rules. Show up. Follow the rules. Work hard. Success will come. His succinct maxims were reassuring. And we did win districts. Then, regionals.

In college, I had the inscrutable Professor Edward Haworth Hoeppner. He was a poet and a pacer. He walked from one side of the room to the other for the entire class period. He ranted rather than lectured and recited verse from memory. He never wrote on the board. Never organized a lecture. What he said often did not make sense. To me. Endless contradictions. He was not concerned. I was concerned, but Professor Hoeppner made me question whether I should be concerned.

97

Jim invited me on a road trip. We were both working hard and our houses were full. It was neat to have alone time penciled in on the calendar. The anticipation kept me sane.

We traveled to Tobermory, Ontario, a little over a five-hour drive from Detroit. We both approached the short road trip as a test of capability—not in a pressure-filled way, but jokingly. Still, it was real. We were in love, but could we spend a big chunk of time together riding in a car, hiking trails, managing downtime. Travel does tend to bring out otherwise hidden quirks of personality. And we would not have our children as buffers or distraction.

The car ride there was talk-heavy. My nervous energy. We reminisced about childhood road trips. Jim and I learned we both had dads who smoked nonstop and who would freak out if a backseat passenger touched the driver's seat. His dad smoked Benson and Hedge's 100's and his mom smoked Carlton's.

Jim shared his mother's family was from Germany; his dad's, from Poland, making him a second generation American. I told him about my dad's dual citizenship. My mom was still a Canadian citizen. I went on and on. I babbled. When I felt us running out of conversation, I proposed that we determine a song that would be our song. And—no worries—I had recorded my suggested options on a cassette tape and brought the tape with me. Jim could easily have determined me psycho at that point.

I would not have blamed him. That said, I was in love. And I was entitled to romance even a silly romantic trope. I still like the songs I selected:

1. "Have a Little Faith in Me," John Haitt
2. "In Your Eyes," Peter Gabriel
3. "Hanging by a Moment," Lifehouse
4. "Iris," The Goo Goo Dolls

I played each song for Jim, and he humored me with a short discussion of their merits. And dismissed them all. We never did decide on a song, but we did dance to "Hanging by a Moment" at our daughter Sophie's wedding several years later.

Our Tobermory motel—and I use the word motel purposefully—was family run, 2-stars, unassuming, and simple. In contrast, Tobermory was and is stunningly beautiful. We followed our planned two-day itinerary. We hiked the Bruce Trail and ate big sandwiches on a rock ledge, our legs dangling over the edge. We took an evening stroll around Little Tug Harbor. Because the exchange rate was so favorable at the time, every time we spent American dollars in a shop, it seemed we received more money back in change. Canadian money. We enjoyed the heady thrill of illusory wealth. We ate dinner at a restaurant next to the Grandview Hotel. The restaurant's signature touch was a two-bite cherry muffin on every plate. Jim and I still talk about those muffins.

The second day, we took a 20-seater Zodiac boat to Flowerpot Island. The term "seater" is generously applied. A seat meant there was room to lean against the inflated side of the boat and hang onto a rope handle. The boat ride was breezy cold. I wore shorts over a bathing suit. My pale white legs quickly covered with goosebumps as we crashed through the water toward the island. Big goosebumps. Other passengers pointed and commented. My legs did look corpse-like. Jim still claimed me as his travel partner. Jim and I explored the island, getting a close look at both flowerpots, two tall rock formations that jut out of Georgian Bay.

During our island hike, we came across a long dock that extended out into a deep inlet of water. As we stood looking at the sun dance on the clear water, I made up a trust exercise. Jim gave me a look. I tend to make up trust exercises. Jim does not. We stripped down to our bathing suits. We both had to jump into the 40-degree water together on the count of three. If we both jumped, without balking, it meant we were destined to be together. Jim liked this idea better than choosing a song. He loves water. And he loves the cold. One. Two. Three. We both jumped. No hesitation. I was happily freezing. Jim, too.

That night, we walked Little Tub Harbor again. Read books. Went to the Little Cove Bakery. Jim purchased cashew brittle; I bought date bars. We split the cost of a bottle of red wine. Again, receiving more dollars back than we paid.

The next morning, we drove home. Both tired. Not too much talking. Compatible quiet.

98

Jim took me to hear Jazz Master Pat Metheny play at the Detroit Opera House. I was in over my head. I do not have a sophisticated ear. As I sat at the Metheny concert, I was confused because, to me, every song sounded the same. In fact, I could not tell when one song ended and the next began. It all seemed like one big song. I had a hard time staying awake. I have no doubt that our Metheny date delayed Jim's eventual marriage proposal by at least twelve months.

99

Jim and I planned a summer trip to explore the American West with the girls. Jim had a van and a pop-up camper. Room for all five girls. Sarah and Sophie begged to stay back. I asked them to call their dad to see if

they could stay with him. Henry agreed. More correctly they said
he agreed.

I had no money for travel. I had to confess this to Jim. He said come
along anyway. I packed my clothes in a brown cardboard box picked
up from the grocery store. I borrowed $100 from Jennifer, so I was not
traveling over 7,000 miles without any ready cash. Another moment of
financial overreach.

Jim, Olivia, Marne, Corrine, and I shared a two-week adventure:
climbing the heights of the Cliff Palace of Mesa Verde, riding mules near
the Grand Canyon, camping on Antelope Island, swimming with sting
rays in San Deigo, enjoying sundaes in a diner, visiting the Monterey
Bay Aquarium, rafting the rapids in Yellowstone, driving while pulling
a camper during a bike road race up the Sienna Nevada mountains,
learning that Jim travels with a ready 10 gallon tank of water just in case,
using said water to cool the van brakes, watching Marne selected for a
demonstration at the Mammoth Site in Hot Springs, camping at the KOA
in the Badlands, and more.

This was a bonding trip. Awkward. Wonderful. When we went horseback
riding in Yellowstone, the guide said that each rider would go by the
name of the horse assigned. My horse's name was "Chunky."
The girls giggled.

Olivia, Marne, and Corrine were good to me—but often kept me at arm's
length, but not out-and-out pushing me away. At the KOA campground in
South Dakota, there was a huge, winding waterslide. The cost: $10.00 a
day per family. Unlimited slides.

Corrine said, "What do they mean by family?"

Olivia asked, "Are we a family?"

Marne piped in, "A family is any group of people who travel together in
a camper."

I exhaled. We paid the $10 fee. No one asked for proof of family. That night, Jim cooked one of the best meals of my life. We only had a box of pasta and a can of tuna left. Tuna pasta. I learned that every meal tastes better when eaten outdoors. Camping.

The next day Jim drove us the remaining 1,100 miles back to Michigan. I did take an early morning driving shift for a few hours, fueled by M&M's. Jim did the lion's share of the trip driving. Meaning almost all of it.

Back in Michigan, Jim returned to an empty house full of fleas—an unexpected situation. He told the girls to stay on the front porch—duffels and bodies out of flea reach. Within minutes the girls were picked up by their mother. I drove back to my apartment, greeted with hugs from Sarah and Sophie. It took me just moments to realize that they had never gone to Henry's house. I noticed mixed nuts in strange places. A hazelnut in the corner of the bathroom. A cashew on the front windowsill. A pecan ground into the shag of the carpet.

I asked about the nuts. The girls admitted to hosting a party. I did not ask any further questions. We moved forward together.

100

Jim had a two-bedroom house on a beautiful pond. Small house. Big yard. A huge family room window overlooked a large pond. Olivia, Marne, and Corrine shared a bedroom with a twin-full bunk bed combination. Closet and dresser.

The girls were on a four days with Mom and then a four days with Dad rotation. I began to watch the girls when Jim was at work. I felt guilt leaving Sarah and Sophie even though they were older. They were mostly okay.

Olivia, Marne, and Corrine and I got along in a stilted kind of way. I was clumsy in my new role. Once when they were on four days with their mom, I cleaned their room. Under beds. The closet. I bought snowflake patterned sheets. New pillows. Soft blue comforters.

The girls returned home to Jim. Olivia liked the cleanliness of the bedroom. She went a step further and covered a tissue box with white paper. Olivia drew snowflakes on the tissue box to match the snowflake sheets. Olivia is a talented artist. Creative. Precise. Perfectionistic.

Jim and I slept in his room on Egyptian cotton sheets given to him by his former mother-in-law. And the bed we slept in was his mother and father's bed.

101

Jim and I took a vacation to Florida with Sophie, Olivia, Marne, and Corrine. My parents had rented us a place on the Gulf of Mexico near their house and near Frank and Jane's townhouse.

The second night after our arrival, Jim and I played Scrabble with Frank. Jane did not play. She was otherwise occupied. Jane had purchased a *Bride's Magazine* and kept interrupting the Scrabble game to show Jim different engagement rings. Very embarrassing. Jim and I were not engaged. I was a poor teacher with two daughters. Jim was a sheriff's deputy with three daughters. Although I was ready to blend our families, I understood that time was needed to consider such a prospect. Jane kept on showing Jim more rings.

The next morning, Jim had a mid-morning scotch. Hard liquor. 10:00 a.m. Not usual. He may have had a second drink. We then took the girls down to the beach. White sand. Aquamarine water. Sophie, Olivia, Marne, and Corrine walked to Jane's townhouse just a little way down the beach, leaving Jim and me alone.

Sunbathing. Towels next to each other. Eyes closed. Silence, except for the waves and seagulls.

Jim asked, "Will you marry me?" No bended knee. No eye contact. A couple of drinks to manage the enormity of it all.

I said, "Yes."

102

Jim and I married in July of 2003. An odd year. Auspicious. We now had five daughters: Sarah, Sophie, Olivia, Marne, and Corrine.

We married in my sister Jennifer's backyard. Thirty guests in attendance. My mom and dad were there. Dad took a zillion pictures. Olivia, Marne, and Corrine wore short white dresses. Sarah and Sophie self-selected their dresses. Sarah wore a long white dress, and Sophie wore a bordello-esque gown. Red, white, and black. I wore a beaded black top and a long black skirt.

When the wedding officiant asked me to put the ring on Jim's finger, I put the ring on Jim's right hand, ring finger. The guests politely laughed an oh-isn't-that-cute laugh. Jim took the ring off of his right hand, ring finger and placed it on his left hand, ring finger. The guests politely laughed again. Public ceremony. Not my forte. The inner bands of both rings were engraved with one word: Tobermory.

Jennifer's husband Scott gave the wedding toast wishing us well and closing with "Sometimes you have to do something twice to get it right."

All five girls did well considering the size of the day. Sophie did complain that an older guest touched her bottom. She was unsure if the contact was intentional.

103

The full-twin bunk bed combination was swapped out for two sets of twin beds—enough room for four: Olivia, Marne, Corrine, and Sophie. Sarah was mostly away at college. And she had a room at Henry's house. Still, Sarah often elected to sleep over. A full house.

The girls started a routine of telling each other scary stories each night. Screams and giggles. Beautiful noise. When it was Corrine's turn to tell a story, she was meticulous about time-stamping her spooky tale. She would say, "At midnight a girl with black hair walked down a dark hallway. At 12:01, she heard a loud noise in the backyard. At 12:02 a.m., the girl fainted when she saw blood. At 12:03 a.m…"

The other girls would eventually interrupt in near unison, "Corrine, stop saying the time!!!"

For my part, I purchased cassettes for the girls to listen to before bedtime: *Spine Chilling Tales of Horror, Tales from the Crypt, Little Evil Things Volume IV, Little Evil Things Volume V, Ozark Tall Tales.* Always ready to spend money on literature.

Anything to nurture new sister bonding. Guilty.

104

When I married Jim, I married into dog ownership: Hannah. Hannah was a mutt, beautifully compact, strong with a rust-colored coat. She had more stamina and determination than any dog I have ever known. Hardwired. Hannah would retrieve a tennis ball for hours. No let up. Back in the day, Hannah ran five miles with me every morning and fourteen miles on a given Sunday—never breaking stride. Never indicating tiredness.

A quintessential Hannah moment: Once during a game of toss and retrieve, Hannah's tennis ball deflected into a roaring campfire. Without thought or hesitation, Hannah chased the ball into the fire. Retrieved it. Unhurt, but with singed hair, Hannah trotted the ball to Jim to toss again.

After Hannah, we adopted an Australian Cattle Dog and named her Carla after a dog in Jim Harrison's novel *True North*. Carla had been removed from her previous home by the police. Carla guarded our children—a shadow dog. Herded them. Every family birthday, Carla sang the "Happy Birthday" song with us—in a quasi-howl-talk.

105

Jim says we melded as a family because we had one bathroom.

Developing routines and traditions also helped. We attended Sarah's soccer games. Sophie's basketball games. Corrine's volleyball games. Elementary graduation ceremonies—where smiles and cooperation were lauded and given primacy. Where Jim and I whispered, "Rebel." We prioritized independence, inquisitiveness, intelligence. We attended plays and musical performances—watching Olivia play the cello. Marne singing a solo. High school graduation parties. Friends blended. Sarah's friend Sara (no "h") came over and led a family tie-dying event. Boyfriends cycled through. Accepted and welcome.

Jennifer and Scott had a cabin in northern Michigan—a ready destination for affordable family travel. And Scott had a boat. At least once a year, we took whoever was available to the cabin. Jim made big meals. I helped. Jim took the girls tubing. I was the spotter, alerting Jim when the girls fell off the tube. Jim gave fast and rough tubing rides. I suspected Jim released some of his life frustrations with each yank on the boat wheel. The girls did not mind. They screamed, "Faster!" The cousin group blended. Cousin Jack and his best friend Roland—so wonderful.

We moved two streets over to a slightly larger house. Three bedrooms. One bathroom. A huge yard—2.18 acres. A large, healthy sycamore tree smack in the back of the yard. Jim built a chicken coup. "An architectural masterpiece," said his wife. He ordered 25 chicks from Murray McMurray Hatchery. The chicks were delivered via mail. Backyard eggs. A great horned owl nested in a tall white pine on the back edge of the property. Not two crows, but the owl felt lucky. Olivia, Marne, and Corrine could walk through the backyard woods to get to their elementary school. Frank sent Jim a check requesting that Jim buy a tractor for himself. Jim did. Jim found solitude on the tractor.

We held the first annual Potocktoberfest, typically the first weekend in October. Potocki + October = Potocktoberfest. Likely an unneeded explanation. Family and Friends. And much food. Pierogies, ham, stuffed cabbage, sausage and sauerkraut. A six-year run.

Florida for Spring Break was an annual trek. Sophie brought her friend Amy. Olivia brought her friend Kendall. Marne brought her friend Ann. More Scrabble with Frank. Jane had three boys, and she relished girl time. When Marne and Corrine were older, Jane took them to a downtown pageant shop to purchase prom dresses. Corrine went with bright purple; Marne, a multicolored gown. Olivia and Sophie were bridesmaids at Sarah's wedding. Beautiful red dresses.

I married into the Potocki Big Pine Key camping tradition. Every Christmas, nearly every year, varying combinations of Jim's siblings and their families gathered at the Big Pine Key Fishing Lodge. Camping. Fishing. Key lime pie on a stick.

The year after Jane and Frank divorced, Frank met Jim and me in Big Pine Key for the winter holiday. I watched with nervousness as his three boys and our girls jumped off the Spanish Channel Bridge. Repeatedly. Bold and joyous. Note: There is now a sign on the bridge that reads, "No jumping off the bridge." Frank helped me through my divorce from Henry. Jim and I tried to help him. And Jane.

Routines. Traditions. One bathroom.

106

Once an inmate who was feeling contemplative asked Jim a question, "How did I end up in jail?"

Jim replied, "Did you ever have a dog?"

"No."

107

Not every new family experience was hunky-dory. Difficult moments were part and parcel of joining our families. Nothing big. Tacit loyalties were sometimes in the room. Respected. Jim and I moved forward together, knowing family was and is always a work in progress.

108

I love words. Jim hails from a Polish father and a German mother— and, by extension, he had a childhood filled with interesting language. Jim introduced me to German words that have no direct English translation—lexical gaps. No one-to-one word translation, such as *schadenfreude* which means feeling pleasure derived from someone else's misfortune.

Jim explained and discussed the meaning of *schadenfreude* with our daughters. The Germanness of the word, the sound of the word carried more weight than the definition. *Schadenfreude*. Our daughters did not want to be guilty of *schadenfreude*.

109

I felt deep connection with my colleagues and school. Jim volunteered to act as food czar of the annual school camping trek. For Jim and me, the camping trip began about four days before the trip departure. We had to prepare food. I use the word "we" loosely because Jim did most all the cooking, freezing, and packing. In my defense, Jim did not enjoy help with kitchen prep. We did, however, go on the camp shopping excursion to Sam's Club together.

One year, at the checkout at Sam's Club, after our three shopping carts full of camping food were rung up, I pulled out the school credit card and gave it to the cashier. The cashier tried the card and then in a loud, surly voice announced, "DECLINED." There was quite a line at the register. Many spectators. I was mortified. And as luck would have it, Jim does not get mortified. He looked directly at the cashier and said, "Try it again." She did. And then she loudly, impatiently announced for a second time, "DECLINED." Jim again countered in a controlled, measured tone, "Try it again." By the third brash and vocal announcement of "DECLINED," I started enjoying the back-and-forth showdown.
It was short-lived though. On the fourth try, the cashier relented.
Instead of publicly shaming us, she politely and quietly asked, "Do you have another card?" Jim immediately gave her another card and paid for the goods.

The bus dropped students and chaperones at the campsite—a large, rustic group spot located on the top of a hill. Heavily wooded. No electricity. The school provided campers with 25 REI tents. Students, in groups of two, were given a set of REI tent instructions, a ground tarp, and tent; then, told to put up their tents. No adult help. Students who figured out how to put up their tents eventually helped other students. And the week of wilderness adventure commenced. The process and frustration of tent construction is a needed life competency, mastery as beautiful as the landscape.

Sarah, Sophie, Olivia, Marne, and Corrine worked various jobs at my school, from volleyball coach to administrative receptionist to summer camp counselor. They were happy. Jim, who cooked 12 turkeys and 10 pounds of potatoes for the annual school Thanksgiving Feast, was mostly happy. I was happy.

110

Chase is the oldest son of Jennifer. Jennifer and Chase. Both lauded oldest siblings. For the record, we love each other and are close. Chase transferred to the school where I taught middle school. He was in my 6th and 7th grade English classes. I felt a little pressure having my oldest sister's oldest child in my classroom.

I knew parents putting an oldest child through middle school tend to worry more about that first child than the siblings that follow. Jennifer was no different. Chase didn't care much for Spanish or math in middle school. He would sometimes skip doing his homework in these classes; instead, he would read unassigned books. Chase loved nonfiction books about Ireland, often 500-plus pages long. Anything Ireland. Jennifer used to fret about his middle school grades in math and Spanish. My theory: Any child reading history tomes for recreational reading is going to be okay. I told Jennifer to relax. Lesson learned: Never tell Jennifer to relax.

Once, in the middle of giving a speech to the whole class, Chase started weeping. Deep crying. With a runny nose, splotchy face, and hiccups of emotion, Chase said to his classmates and me, "My gerbil died last night. Giving this speech feels meaningless." I told Chase to breathe, sit down, and relax. Chase accepted the relax directive much better than my sister Jennifer.

In Chase's very first middle school basketball game, he was fouled and called to the free throw line. I clapped and cheered, "Go, Chase!" Jennifer sat next to me a mess of emotion. Chase missed the first shot. An airball. Jennifer seemed to curl inward, unable to manage the moment. Luckily, Chase sank the second shot. When I looked over though, Jennifer was crying. Tears of joy, but tears that welled from a place deep within.

111

I have a bad habit. If Jim pauses or happens to breathe near the end of a sentence when he is talking, I jump in and complete his sentence for him. I cannot help myself. It is not impulsivity. It feels more like a live action fill-in-the blank moment. Exciting for me, but admittedly rude. Unintentional though. The transgression: To encroach on the utterance of another uninvited. I am guilty.

112

Jim quietly left the Niagara Falls campground. Walked away. Olivia, Marne, and Corrine slept soundly. I had been up for hours. Reading. I typically woke up each day around 3:00 a.m. to have some alone time. Read. Exercise. Grade papers. In a large family, alone time needs to be intentionally orchestrated.

Giving Jim a 5-minute head start, I followed him. I was not in the habit of tailing Jim. We appreciated time and space apart, our trust absolute. But that morning I followed him. I stayed a good distance back, knowing Jim is hyper-aware of his surroundings. He was headed somewhere. After about a mile, Jim turned into a building. I kept going. I peeked into the window of the building. Jim was in line buying a bagel.

I quickly turned to head back to the campground. I took a few steps back toward the campground. I determined that my stalker behavior was unacceptable. Confession required. I wheeled back around and entered the bagel shop. Jim, now seated, looked up surprised.

I said, "I followed you."

He said, "Creepy."

I replied, "I know."

We managed to laugh away the oddity of the moment and walked back to camp. Jim jokingly giving sidelong glances. Our road trip was just at its beginning: Niagara Falls to Mt. Washington to Maine to New Brunswick to Nova Scotia. My dad and mom were meeting us in New Brunswick.

To this point in my life, I had never tried coffee, beer, cigarettes, and marijuana. I had also never tried lobster. I was looking forward to trying lobster in Maine, an authentic lobster roll. Our daughter Marne would spend a college summer working on a lobster boat, an adventure many years down the road.

That day, we enjoyed a soaking received on the Maid of the Midst boat ride and were awed by the sound and power of the Falls. After a grilled cheese dinner at the campground, I went to bed early. The drive to the next campground at the foot of Mt. Washington was in New Hampshire. Ten hours away.

113

The next morning, Jim drove first. I drove second, a good five-hour stint. I was gaining experience towing the camper. We stopped to fill up with gas. I asked Jim if he wanted anything from the gas station market.

He said, "Nonpareils."

I said, "What is that?"

"Little circles of chocolate with tiny beads of sugar on top. Like, Sno Caps at the movie theater." Oddly, the gas station had a boutique bag of locally made nonpareils. Jim drove for the final hour, headed to the campground.

A few minutes after leaving the gas station, I lost my eyesight. I did not say anything immediately. I am stoic and dumb like that. But I caved. "Jim, I can't see anything," I shared in a matter-of-fact voice. No need for histrionics.

"What do you mean?"

"I cannot see."

While Jim was pulling over, my eyesight returned. "It's okay. I can see now." My sight had come back. I received a sidelong glance from Jim. This was turning into the trip of sidelong glances. I gave him a smile. He resumed driving to Mt. Washington. When we were just a mile or so from our destination, Jim handed me the map and asked for help getting to the campground. I do not remember much after that.

Jim later told me he made it to the campground. He ran into the front office and said, "I believe my wife is having a stroke. I need to use your phone." Jim remained calm. The office staff were unsettled.

An ambulance arrived shortly. Local volunteers. I have flashes of memory of the EMT's removing me from of the van. I protested, worried that I was not wearing shoes. I remember them taking scissors to my clothes. Then, I slumped into unconsciousness again.

Jim said, "Give her high flow oxygen." The EMT's complied. They loaded me in the ambulance and headed for the area hospital. Once there, the ER doctor, in a Scottish brogue, explained the pros and cons of giving me Tissue Plasminogen Activator (tPA), a drug that dissolves clots and restores blood flow. Jim gave his consent. I am forever grateful. From the area hospital, I was transported by ambulance to the Dartmouth-

Hitchcock Medical Center (DHMC). Jim and the girls followed in the van, still towing the camper.

I achieved a couple minutes of consciousness that night. A DHMC neurologist kept loudly asking me to move my right arm. Shout-talking at me. "Move your right arm." My brain acknowledged the request, but my right side did nothing. Again, I heard the loud request: "Move your right arm."

My brain was thinking, "Why is he asking me to do something that I cannot do. I am unable to move my right arm."

"Move your right arm" was again uttered with urgency and volume. With attitude, I opened my eyes. I made intentional eye contact with the neurologist. I then reached over with my left arm and shook my right arm. The neurologist smiled at my workaround. Jim smiled. I slipped into unconsciousness again.

Olivia, Marne, and Corrine spent the night in the DHMC parking lot. Jim stayed with me as needed, called my sister Jennifer who would share news with Sarah and Sophie, and returned to the van to reassure the girls, and collapsed for a needed nap.

114

I woke up the next morning. Tired. My periphery vision was wonky; otherwise, my body and mind seemed okay. Jim was there. He held my hand.

"What happened?"

"You had a stroke, an ischemic attack. Likely caused by a congenital heart defect. The doctor suspects that you have an opening between the two upper chambers of your heart. Usually, this opening closes soon after birth. Your opening did not close."

He told me I was scheduled for a transesophageal echocardiogram to confirm the diagnosis. There was a wrinkle.

"You are pregnant." I felt an immediate surge of joy, quickly tempered by the knowledge that my body had experienced trauma yesterday.

Dad and Mom arrived at DHMC that afternoon. Olivia, Marne, and Corrine were still living in the parking lot. My parents booked a hotel for the girls, taking turns with Jim to provide them entertainment and breaks—mostly swimming in the hotel pool and taking a few trips to the Ben and Jerry's Ice Cream store in Waterbury, Vermont. Interspersed with downtime. Waiting.

I have never seen Jim cry. Olivia, Marne, and Corrine tell me that Jim cried during the drive from the Mt. Washington local hospital to Dartmouth-Hitchcock Medical Center.

115

I elected to have the transesophageal echocardiogram without sedation, concerned the sedation might hurt the baby. In layman's terms, the procedure required a tube being gently shoved down my throat to take pictures of my heart—enabling a determination of problem and next steps. I said the ABCs in my head to remain calm and to avoid gagging.

The next step would happen in September: A Patent Foramen Ovale (PFO) closure. In layman's terms, putting a screen over the hole in my heart, so flesh would grow over the hole. As luck would have it, the best heart doctor in the country who does this procedure worked at a hospital a few miles from our Michigan house. I was placed on medication, an anti-coagulant, and sent home. In total, a 4-day stay at the DHMC.

116

I had a miscarriage. My periphery vision returned to normal. My first appointment with the heart doctor was still over a month away. I taught classes that summer. Life felt somewhat normal.

Our eventual visit with the heart doctor was disconcerting. Jim and I waited in the waiting room. We were next told to wait in an examination room. After a time, the doctor entered the room with my file. As he made a quick review of my file, we waited patiently.

When the doctor looked up, he said with professional bravado, "I could have saved that baby." I was stunned. The doctor said a couple of other things and confirmed the date of my PFO closure procedure. He exited.

I turned to Jim, giving my immediate impression, "He is an arrogant asshole."

Jim did not disagree. He instead asked, "Do you want the world renowned, arrogant doctor or a competent, personable doctor doing your procedure?

I replied, "The arrogant asshole."

The routine PFO procedure went well. I passed all metrics on my follow-up visits. Hole fixed. I still have not had a lobster roll, but I did become pregnant again three months later.

117

At Christmas, Sarah brought her fiancé Eric to share in the opening of gifts ritual. During her young adult years, Sarah did not do holidays well. Residual divorce baggage.

While the whole Potocki family watched, it was Sarah's turn to open a gift. She became self-conscious. Tears started to gather. Distressed, she stood up and yelled, "Fuck all of you." She exited the house with a door slam. And went to sit by the chicken coop to cry. Jim, Sophie, Olivia, Marne, Corrine, and I all looked over at Eric, hoping he was still going to marry Sarah. He did.

118

Someone knocked on the front door, prompting Carla to bark loudly and to bite at the front window. Carla looked crazy mean when she did this. I felt safe with Carla.

I peeked out the window. A young man holding a chicken stood on our porch. I told Carla to be quiet. I opened the door.

"May I help you?"

"Is Corrine home?" I thought he would at least reference the chicken in his arms.

"Corrine is not home right now," I said. He frowned.

"I caught this chicken. I think it is yours."

My guess: The young man took the chicken from the coup, giving him a reason to come to our front door, hoping to talk to Corrine.

"I'll meet you in the backyard, and we can put the chicken back in the coup." I gave him points for ingenuity and for his willingness to hold a chicken. In the winter no less.

119

A common aspect of human relationships: each member of the relationship will undoubtedly possess a certain habit, inability, trait, or patter that drives the other member of the relationship crazy.

Cohabitating couples—even those who are wildly compatible, wildly in love—irk each other sometimes. There is always something.

Map reading, for example. If my dad asked my mom to read a map when on a road trip, the car immediately hushed. My siblings and I knew an argument was coming. Mom was not directionally wired. We once ended up in Brownsville, Virginia when we were headed to Brownsville, Maryland. In Mom's defense, the two Brownsvilles are separated by just 22 miles. Still, Dad could not resist announcing, "Mary, you took us to the wrong state."

My towel folding annoys Jim. I fold towels in a square. A loose square. A sloppy square. Good enough. The towels sit stacked in the linen closet without complaining. Jim though—with his Air Force folding training— will often refold the towels. He is insanely talented at towel folding. So is Olivia.

But Jim has his thing. A large green water cup. A tumbler. It sits by the kitchen sink. I once washed it. He said, "Who touched my cup?" His relationship with the cup is exclusive. I am not supposed to touch the cup.

Interestingly, Jim and I both share a personality trait that drives the other crazy: Neither of us is good at asking for help. Jim was once having a coughing fit. I said, "Let me get you a glass of water."

He barked back, "I'll get my own water!" Help rejected. He was probably worried I was going to touch his green cup.

120

I am help-avoidant as well. Once Jim and I shared a quick evening out at a local pizzeria before he worked an 11-3 shift at the jail. We split the house special. A Green Pizza. Mozzarella, spinach, and garlic. An ordinary, wonderful meal.

That evening, after Jim had gone to work, I started feeling sick. I was five months pregnant, so I thought maybe the spiciness of the pizza was to blame. I felt nauseous. And had a deep ache on my right side. I thought, "Maybe I have an appendicitis. I should go get this checked." I dressed and drove myself to the emergency hospital.

The medical personnel ran tests. It was determined I had appendicitis—immediate removal required. I asked questions, including, "Is it okay to have surgery while I am pregnant?" I learned the hospital had a whole antenatal section for patients who have surgery while pregnant. I was wheeled to a pre-operative waiting area. It was at this point I called Jim.

"Hey, Jim. Everything is okay. I am at the hospital. I am in the queue for an appendectomy. Surgery will happen sometime this morning. Fairly soon. I am told the baby will be fine."

Jim was less than thrilled that I had not called earlier. Like before I headed to the hospital. He was miffed. I was guilty but unintentionally so. He would get there as soon as possible.

The wait for surgery was uneventful—although something curious happened. I did not think it was curious at the time. The waiting area was quiet. I was thinking about the surgery. I was thinking about Jim. I was thinking about the baby.

I was lying there doing all this thinking when a doctor came over and said, "There is just one more check to make." He put on some sterile gloves and proceeded to give me a quick rectal exam.

In my head, I said, "Really."

To the doctor, I said, "Thank you."

Now, years later, I think, "Who was this guy? Was he even a doctor?"

Immediately before surgery, they collected my jewelry. My wedding ring. As they took my wedding ring, I felt my first moment of panic. Fear.

I should have called Jim earlier.

121

I lied about my due date. A white lie. The doctor calculated my due date: August 29. My mind said, "No, that date has baggage." Two things: 1. My ex-husband's birth date. 2. School was scheduled to begin in early September. I did not want to take a maternity leave and force students into a substitute situation. I changed the due date to August 15. I told work it was the 15th. I told Jim it was the 15th.

I was 42. I underwent genetic testing because of my "advanced maternal age." I learned I was having a boy. Our five daughters were relieved. Sophie said, "Thank God, I am not getting another sister."

I have a fixation with the name Ignatius, a character from *A Confederacy of Dunces*, a novel on my top ten books of all time list. Ignatius means "fiery one." Major cool points. To me, Ignatius is a perfect name, and I do not even know if I believe in perfection. I have sometimes felt perfection in an imperfect moment though. Anyway, I thought, "If I ever have a son, I will name him Ignatius. His nickname will be Iggy."

Jim, however, announced that he wanted to name the baby after his father—Tadeusz Casimir Potocki— who was a veteran of WWII and who unexpectedly passed away when Jim was in 7th grade. My infatuation with the name Ignatius suddenly seemed a little superficial.

122

On the morning of August 15th, my water broke when I stepped out of bed. Jim and I rounded up the girls and called my parents who had come into town for the birth. We would keep them posted.

I was calm, but I did remember the mental pact I had made with God when I was pregnant with Sophie: "If you give me a healthy baby, I will never have another child." A Faustian bargain. I was young and dumb.

As Jim and I checked in the maternity ward, the nurse announced, "Hmmm—due on the 29th. You are two weeks early." I looked at Jim. He noted the discrepancy, but he didn't question me. I was in labor.

Sarah, Sophie, Olivia, Marne, and Corrine arrived to the spacious birthing room. A long window bench ran the length of one wall— discretely located behind my gurney. When the doctor checked on me, I still had a measure of privacy. I told the doctor that I delivered my first two babies moments after I reached four centimeters dilation. The doctor looked at me incredulously. I was at four centimeters now. The doctor hesitated but said, "I am going to deliver another baby and be right back." I think we have time.

Before the doctor reached the door, the nurse said with urgency, "The baby is coming now." The doctor spun back around.

I looked over at the girls and said, "The baby is coming. Please leave now." The girls exited.

In less than five minutes, Tadeusz "Teddy" Potocki was born. Jim cut the umbilical cord. I called out to the girls, "You can come back now. The baby is here."

The girls still tease me about how calm and polite I was during Teddy's delivery. No drama. After I was moved to a private room, my parents came to visit. They took a picture of each of the girls holding Teddy. Jennifer came to visit.

Jim ended up taking a paternity leave to care for Teddy, so I could begin the school year with my 6th and 7th grade classes. My school asked me to submit a doctor's note to be able to return without taking a maternity leave. That seemed an unnecessary requirement to me. An overreach. Jim said, "Pick your battles." I submitted the doctor's note.

123

The first time I married it was in the county courthouse. A spartan ceremony. The second time I married it was in my sister's backyard—a comparatively huge event. Thirty guests.

When Sarah became engaged, she immediately purchased *Bride's Magazine* and began wedding planning. Sarah wanted a big wedding. One hundred and fifty guests. She was given a modest budget—we had four other daughters at home. A new baby. Wise not to set an extravagant precedent. To her credit, Sarah was a genius at researching, budgeting, selecting a venue, determining colors, flowers, and theme—finding friends-and-family discounts on many details, including booking a colleague of Jim's for the DJ.

Sarah and I did have one wedding planning argument: chair covers. To me, the uncovered chairs in the hall looked fine. They made Sarah cry. Tears over banquet hall chairs? I cannot remember the exact price, but the dollar amount felt incongruous even when compared to the startling cost of a wedding cake. I did not immediately relent, but I eventually caved. Sarah ordered white chair covers with deep crimson bows.

When I walked into the banquet hall following Sarah's wedding ceremony, I was struck by the beauty of the room. That night, I ended up learning that I loved big weddings. The planning and expense no longer felt frivolous. It was wonderful to set aside an evening to pamper friends and family with good food and entertainment—to relax and celebrate that we were all together sharing space, acknowledging a significant, happy occasion. A welcome time-out, allowing attendees to pause together and simply be in the moment, consciously and conscientiously marking time.

124

Back in the day, before blow dryers, I had a teacher in high school— Mrs. Solomon—who said no student in her classroom was allowed to come to her class with wet hair because she disliked the smell of wet hair and shampoo fragrance. I had Mrs. Solomon first period and was often reprimanded for my dampness. Mrs. Solomon had a "my space, my rules" approach to classroom governance. No invitation for discussion. I thought the hair rule unfair but respected that Mrs. Solomon crafted her own world with her own rules.

As a parent, I did have rules, but I was inconsistent across children. I did adhere to one parenting rule always: No baby talk. No baby talk even to babies. I never said blankie, snuggle wuggles, paci, or sleepy-pie. I couldn't pull it off. No one spoke baby talk to me. Heck, no one even spoke to me when I was growing up. Okay, slight hyperbole. But not by much. Parent baby talk felt risky. I rationalized: I was raising adults, not children.

Jennifer was a master at mellifluous mommy-talk when raising her two sons. She would call to her youngest son, "Where's my blueberry boy?" Her mommy-voice was filled with a love that balked at dignity. It was hard not to be jealous. Jane had a parent-language between herself and her young sons. Not baby talk, but a Jane-ian vernacular filled with a love that inspired exceptional vocabulary, a want of learning and adventure, along with cache of individual nicknames. Jimmy Puddle Feet, Jimmy Swimmy, Maxaroni (a riff on Macaroni), Paxman (a riff on Pacman), Stevie-Sweetie.

I did not get that piece of genetic code.

125

I had a student named Michael. He knew baseball statistics forwards and backwards. He loved numbers—even more, a love for calculating numbers. Michael stayed after English class one day and sidled up to my desk.

Michael informed me, "You drink at least two Diet Cokes a day. If you stop drinking Diet Coke, you will save between $365-$730 per year. Two Diet Cokes per day costs about $1 a day—and that's only if you buy in bulk at Sam's Club or Costco. If you buy your Diet Coke from the gas station, my estimate is too low."

At the time, Teddy was a year old. Still not sleeping through the night. Diet Coke had become a night-time go-to, a morning pick-me-up.

I gave up Diet Coke while pregnant. Post-pregnancy, I overcorrected and began drinking the caffeine-laced drink with abandon. Michael had gravely underestimated my Diet Coke habit—consumption rate, cost, and need.

126

Teddy's first sentence was "Don't tell me what."

When Teddy's preschool teacher wanted him to put his coat on, she said, "Teddy, do not put your coat on." He immediately and happily put his coat on.

His teacher would also say, "Teddy, don't you dare give me a hug good-bye." Teddy immediately and happily gave her a hug good-bye.

Jim can tie expert-level knots. A needed skill in a large household. I can tie shoes. When I tied Teddy's first pair of lace-up shoes for the first time, Teddy stared at the neat bows. He then spoke one word: "Butterflies." I loved that moment. I mentally relive it often. I tell the story too often.

127

I am not a touchy-feely person. Once, I participated in a three-day seminar on giftedness—professional development and certification. The three days included much instruction and a few bonding activities. I participated fully.

At the close of the training, the facilitator stood at the exit, hugging each participant as we departed. As I approached the facilitator, she leaned in for a hug. I said, "Oh no, I do not do that." I offered my hand.

My colleague Patrick, who was behind me in line, laughed. He said, "I did not think refusal was an option."

I disrupted the flow of hugs. The facilitator shifted to handshakes.

128

We did not have a television in our household until Teddy was three years old. My sister and her husband were replacing their 50-inch television with something smaller. Downsizing. Jim and I didn't want a television, but this was free.

In general practice, we did not allow young Teddy to watch television. We did not want to corrupt his brain—nor ours. There were nights though when both Jim and I came home tired from work—usually Friday night and we wanted to just sit. The 50-inch screen called to us.

We asked ourselves, "What is appropriate programming to watch with a three-year-old?" We discussed, rationalized, and determined the answer: Professional Bull Riding (PBR). CBS Sports happened to televise the U.S. bull riding season which runs from January to May. For just a few weeks, we fell into the habit of watching rodeo tournaments with Teddy—*Monster Energy Bucking Battle*, *Frontier Communications Iron Cowboy*, and *Last Cowboy Standing*.

As luck would have it, a projector bulb exploded and our brief lapse into televised Americana was over. For the next seven years, no television.

129

I dragged 3-year-old Teddy to yet another end-of-day faculty meeting. I had a new 64-box of Crayola crayons and some paper to keep him busy. During my meeting, Teddy did not color. He spent the entire meeting peeling the paper off each crayon and then breaking the crayon. At the end of the meeting, I happily helped Teddy pick up his broken crayons.

As we were cleaning up, my math teacher colleague Ms. Chu came over to me. She was weeping. Big tears streaming down her face. Ms.

Chu cried, "I never let my children break their crayons." Her crying continued, "It was so beautiful to watch Teddy break the crayons. And you did not yell at him once. I should have let my children break their crayons." Crayon-breaking. Good parenting? Not sure.

130

My dad purchased eight grave plots in Santa Rosa Cemetery. He was not dying, not even close. Advanced planning. He referred to it as "The Park." He proceeded to develop the property. A stone border was installed around the perimeter of the plots. He added a doublewide headstone for Mom and himself. Later, a marble bench with all the names of his grandchildren engraved around the seating surface. Teddy's name "Tadeusz" was a late add. Dad did not expect that I would have another baby at 42. The cemetery sits just a few blocks from the Gulf of Mexico. I thought his advanced planning was a little strange.

131

When Sophie married Devon, she received the same modest budget as Sarah. No increase for inflation, but I did not balk at chair covers. I even went slightly over budget by getting a surprise bakery-made chocolate groom's cake in the shape of an Atlanta Braves jersey decorated with the #10—the number of my new son-in-law's favorite player. Chipper Jones. Teddy was the ringbearer.

Both Henry and Jim walked Sophie down the aisle—an act of maturity and love not lost on my girlfriend Laurie. She made a point of talking to Henry about it. I appreciated the gesture as well, but I did not talk to Henry. I had not talked to Henry since our divorce. I do know he became a professional golfer, and he has a strong relationship with both Sarah and Sophie. And he remarried.

Near the end of the wedding, I watched my sister Jennifer dance to "Brick House" by the Commodores. She dances to this song at every family wedding. I will never find the comfort she has on the dance floor. Jealous.

132

I had a colleague, a school psychologist, who used the term "both-and" often. During conflict resolution, she worked to bring students in disagreement to a both-and perspective, rather than an either-or stalemate. I'll make up a scenario: EITHER Student A is wrong for excluding Student B from a lunchtime game of basketball OR Student B requires exclusion because his silly antics disrupt game play.

After listening to each student's version of events, the school psychologist would announce, "What we have here is a both-and situation." BOTH students are correct: Student A should not exclude Student B from the game AND Student B should be excluded because his silly antics disrupt game play. From this both-and quandary, she worked with students toward problem-solving and resolution. She used the both-and strategy with such dexterity that one would think she invented the methodology. She taught me that both-and is a thing.

I was often guilty of either-or thinking. I was, for example, a speech judge every forensics season. Some of my hardest bouts of rigid thinking occurred when judging oratory tournaments. In these tournaments, the speaker's ideas and the presentation of those ideas were both weighted. As a result, the student with the best thinking was not always awarded the trophy. I felt conflicted. I wanted to shout during the awards ceremony, "EITHER the best thinking wins OR this tournament is a sham!" My heart still bleeds a little.

An absolutist position though is naive. A compelling idea uttered with a lack of confidence or without clarity often goes unheard. BOTH the ability to think well AND the ability to present well impact the life of an idea. And life. For that matter.

133

I sent three-year-old Teddy to summer camp. At camp, each age group was given a bird name. Teddy was a Chickadee. My son was a Chickadee. Weirdly thrilling. I felt an avian-fueled joy when I dropped Teddy at camp on Day 1.

When I picked Teddy up from summer camp on Day 1, his counselor pulled me aside and said, "Teddy wet his pants today." I nearly said, "No, he didn't," as the counselor handed me a plastic bag with Teddy's wet clothes inside.

Requirement: Chickadees had to be potty-trained. NO exceptions. I didn't give this rule a second thought because fastidious Teddy hadn't been in diapers for nearly a year. Dream child. Potty-trained in 48-hours at 25 months.

As soon as I put Teddy in the car, he fell fast asleep. I rationalized. Teddy must have wet his pants because of the newness of the camp experience. Normal, natural excitement.

When I picked Teddy up from summer camp on Day 2, his counselor pulled me aside and said, "Teddy wet his pants again today." And the counselor used a tone with me. A tone that indicated that camp parents baldly and routinely lied about bathroom readiness.

I became defensive. "Listen, Teddy has driven to Florida and back twice this year. No accidents. And sometimes he had to wait until the next exit which was miles away." My proclamation fell flat as she handed me a second plastic bag containing Teddy's wet clothes. As soon as I put

Teddy in the car, he fell fast asleep. I rationalized. Teddy must have wet his pants because the camp counselor was overhydrating him.

When I dropped Teddy off at camp on Day 3, I said gently, maybe with a hint of tone, "Please do not overhydrate Teddy today." About halfway through camp on Day 3, the Camp Director phoned our house. I was not home. No one was home. When I did arrive home, I listened to the waiting message on our answering machine: "Mrs. Potocki, Teddy wet his pants today at camp. This is his third accident. Three strikes. He can try camp again next year. Today is his last day."

I felt a deep anger and a deep hurt. I was also confused. Why was Teddy wetting his pants? I blamed the camp. They—the camp counselors—must be doing something wrong. When I picked Teddy up from summer camp on Day 3, I asked for clarification. "Can you please explain to me when Teddy is wetting his pants? Is he getting lost in play and forgetting? Do you remind campers to take bathroom breaks? Is this happening during nap time? Are there an adequate number of bathrooms? Are the bathrooms dimly lit, scary places?"

The counselor explained, "It is really quite odd. Teddy asks to go to the bathroom. We take him to the bathroom. Teddy goes into the bathroom and then comes out with wet pants." The counselor then proceeded to hand me a third plastic bag of wet clothes. I loaded Teddy in the car.

As soon as I put Teddy in the car, he fell fast asleep. I was numb. My son. Age three. Ex-Chickadee. Expelled from summer camp. Once in our driveway, Teddy woke up. He sleepily whispered, "I have to go potty." Leaving the car door open, I rushed Teddy into the house, took him into the bathroom, plopped him down in front of the toilet. I caught myself as I reflexively started to pull his pants down.

In that second, realization hit me hard. Teddy was potty-trained. Impeccably so. Problem: He didn't know how to pull his pants down. I never taught him. I never allowed him this responsibility.

I didn't send Teddy back to camp that summer. He was ready. I was not.
I needed time to wallow. How else had I unwittingly crippled my son's
chances of success and independence?

134

I was in a Board meeting. My phone lit up. It was a text message from
my daughter Sophie: "I am in labor. Come now." Sophie and Devon
lived in Toledo—about an hour away.

I left the meeting. Drove directly to Toledo. By the time I arrived, I had
a new granddaughter. When Sophie handed her to me, she said, "I'd like
you to meet Mary Colleen." I teared up. I took Mary Colleen in my arms.
My name had never looked so beautiful.

135

Sarah calls me nearly every day. When she is sitting in a car waiting
for my grandson Grayson to finish swimming practice. Or waiting for
my granddaughter Jillian to finish soccer practice. Or waiting for my
grandson Jack to finish baseball practice. Or when she is on her commute
home from work. Or when she is walking the dog.

I am not a phone person. My phone rings.

"Hello, Sarah."

"Hi, Mom. What are you doing?"

"I am sitting on the couch."

"I am waiting for Gray to finish practice."

"Okay."

"Mom, make an effort."

"Okay."

"I am your daughter."

"Okay."

Sarah eventually gets exasperated with me and ends the phone call. I still loved her phone call. And I hope she calls again tomorrow.

My children tell me I have never had a phone conversation with them that lasts longer than two minutes. They say this as if it were a bad thing.

136

Jim and I do not fight often. We have the typical marital moments of disagreement—and, on rare occasions, a few days of disagreement. We are well matched, except for one splotch of consistent incompatibility: driving.

Jim hugs the centerline when he drives, and I lean on the right shoulder when I drive. Jim is an exceptional driver. A limousine driver in his younger days. His fire station had him drive the fire engine any time there was black ice or messy road conditions. Never had an accident. Still, I cannot help myself when I feel the car is too close to the center line. I involuntarily flinch. I reflexively grip the arm rest. I do not have trust issues. I have control issues.

I am not a good passenger in any car. With any driver. Jim and I have managed this area of incompatibility, most often, with success. The best remedy to date: I sit in the backseat.

137

When Teddy was four-years old he had to sit for an IQ test in order to continue in his elementary school for gifted students. Young Teddy was asked which two of three pictures matched: a turtle, an alligator, and a light. Teddy said, "Alligator and light."

The tester said, "Wrong—the turtle and alligator are both reptiles."

Teddy replied, "An alligator needs sunlight to live. An alligator does not need a turtle to live. I pick alligator and light."

I liked Teddy's answer.

138

My life became crowded. Good crowded, like winning the Guinness world record for the most people fit into a Volkswagen Beetle. Fifty-seven. Or most people fit into a Mini Cooper. Twenty-nine. Or phone booth. Twenty-two. Note: The jury is still out with regards to the phone booth. The record ranges between 22-25 people. A lack of agreement on official results. Official, a tricky word. Crowdedness can cause crankiness. And I can be cranky—especially after 5:00 p.m.

Teddy often had to accompany me to faculty meetings. Start time: 3:30 p.m. The start of fading time. I set him up in a back corner with paper and crayons. He happily, quietly drew the length of the meeting. No crayon breaking this time. The meeting ran late: 5:20 p.m. My mood meter was in the red zone. Ted was content. I was done.

At the close of the meeting, a colleague approached Teddy. She looked at his drawing and said, "What is that? A car? A plane? The Batmobile?"

I was tired. I was tonal. I said to my colleague, "Please do not guess what Teddy is drawing. You are crushing his imagination. Let him— if he chooses—tell you what it is." Yikes. My colleague made a quick getaway.

139

Once when I attended Teddy's parent-teacher conferences, the classroom walls were filled with student work. As I surveyed the room, one wall made me cringe: The Wall of Favorites. Teddy's teachers had each student fill out a list of favorites. Favorite food. Favorite toy. Favorite book. Favorite sport. Favorite color. Favorite holiday. I thought, "Why not ask favorite parent?"

Jim should have been there to kick me under the table. He was working a double shift. I told Teddy's teachers to never make him pick out a favorite anything again. Ever. And I went on. I told them favorite-thinking was reductive thinking. I questioned, "Why does a student have to have a favorite anything? Or for that matter, a least favorite anything? Choosing one as favorite immediately discounts others—ranks them as lesser. Unnecessary."

I was tired that evening. When I am tired, small things become big things. I eventually stopped myself. I awkwardly tried to redirect the conversation with compliments and pleasantries for the remainder of the discussion.

These were two fantastic teachers. As the meeting progressed, it was evident that Teddy was thriving and his teachers adored him—me, not so much. I was definitely not going to be voted the favorite parent-teacher conference of the day.

140

One condition of parenthood caught me by surprise: A child is born with a distinct imprint of personality. I naively thought a baby came into the world an empty vessel personality-wise—just bones, body parts, and a blank brain.

Nope. Sarah was born screaming with a leap-before-looking personality, likes a little drama and is tough as nails. Sophie was born with a calm, disarming, charismatic personality—friends and family want her in the room. Olivia was born with a hardy streak of rule-making and order-making and self-sufficiency and artistic talent. Marne has always had a heart that felt more than other hearts, fortunately coupled with no-nonsense strength. Corrine was born with a social capacity for shape-shifting—comfortably and easily acting as a mirror for others, sometimes elusive in her sharing of self.

Teddy was born a contrary child. Not contrary in a bad way. He simply does not like being told what to do. Born that way. When teaching toddler Teddy his alphabet, he figured out quickly that I wanted him to say the letters in order: A, B, C, D, E and so on. In response to my excited promptings to say the alphabet, Teddy would respond with a grin, "H, J, E, C, X," but never in order. To date, Teddy has never said the ordered alphabet aloud in my presence.

141

Marne once worked in the woods of North Carolina. She was a counselor at a wilderness therapy program for teens. I received a text from Marne one evening. No words. Just a video of a huge black bear walking about the woods. Quite beautiful. Still, if Marne were the videographer, she was way too close to this animal. About five Honda Accord lengths away, if that. I was cool in my text reply: "A little scary. Stay safe. Bear spray. Bear horn. I hope all is going well. I love you much." Marne did not immediately reply to my message. I eventually learned she was not eaten by the bear when she texted a week later.

Marne is a wonderful adult, and she was a fairly easy teen. Occasionally we had philosophical disagreements. Teen Marne would firmly tell me, "If I don't tell you about something it is not a lie."

I would follow her assertion with a parental harangue about truthfulness: "Marne, there are two types of lies: lies of commission and lies of omission. A lie of commission occurs when you out-and-out tell me something that is not true. A lie of omission occurs when you do not share what is true even though you know the truth. The lie is in the omitted detail that you do not say."

Teen Marne would reply, "No, that doesn't sound like a lie to me."

Teen Marne won nearly every disagreement we ever had. Why? She simply did not engage in parent-daughter conflict. She remained calm. Composed. I ended up looking foolish, unbalanced—even when I had a valid point.

The power of calm is disarming. Marne is good at disarming.

142

When Teddy was about seven years old, he went through a fearful phase. Jim and I decided that exposure to risk would help him overcome his fears, so we took him canoeing in a Louisiana bayou filled with alligators. Wrinkle: No alligators showed up.

We then took him to the Global Wildlife Center in Folsom, Louisiana for an open-wagon tour during which visitors had the opportunity to hand feed giraffes, camels, elands, and bison that roamed about the expansive grounds. All was good until the tour guide cautioned, "Do not feed the zebras. They will bite your fingers off. I repeat: Do not feed the zebras. You will lose your fingers." Teddy was rattled. The zebras did aggressively stick their heads into the wagon, but no fingers were lost.

Teddy had mixed feelings about the experience, but he learned that he could survive the discomfort of zebra terror.

143

My siblings and I all ended up college-educated, law-abiding, and employed. My dad, a strict parent, placed a check in the win column. Mission accomplished. As a Marine, my dad took pride that all of his children, after first marriages, eventually married a veteran.

On a trip to Big Pine Key, Florida one year, Jim and I decided to stop by Panama City for a quick visit with my parents. During that visit we went to Walmart. When visiting my parents, Walmart was part of the routine. At Walmart, Dad bought Teddy his first bike, a two-wheeler bike with training wheels. Dad helped Teddy learn to ride that bike, yelling "Go, Deucie!" with pure joy—no edge of strictness. After the visit, we proceeded to Big Pine Key to camp.

144

As soon as we arrived at the campground, Teddy decided he wanted to learn to ride his new two-wheeler—without training wheels. The day was beautiful. Teddy had a long stretch of hard sand in front of our camper. He tried many times to get going but was not finding success. It was clear he did not want me to teach him how to ride the bike. If I even gently whispered advice, Teddy yelled in frustration, "Don't tell me what!" Teddy kept attempting to ride. Eventually tears were streaming down his cheeks, but he kept trying and falling. I respectfully kept my distance.

A college-aged camper was sitting on the beach nearby watching Teddy's stubborn independence. He stood up and walked over to Teddy. He told Teddy how cool his bike was. He told Teddy he remembered learning to ride his bike. He asked Teddy if he could give him a little help. Teddy—without making eye contact—nodded yes.

The young man held the back of the bike giving Teddy time to situate his feet on the pedals. After a few assisted launches and some coaching, Teddy was able to balance himself and get started on his own. The young man smiled a huge smile, gave Teddy a few cheers of encouragement, and ambled away. Teddy spent the remainder of the day joyfully riding back and forth along the beachfront. I am pretty sure a part of his happiness was owning his success without parent help. Without my help.

I have sometimes regretted not speaking to the young man who helped Teddy learn to ride his bike. I should have spoken up and thanked him. I understood though that my thanking the young man, in the moment, might have taken something from Teddy, compromising a relationship he made, the help he accepted, and the success he found without me.

145

After a few days of camping, I received a call from Mom: Dad fell down on his way into a Waffle Shoppe for coffee. An ambulance came. A brain tumor found. Biopsy required. We left Big Pine Key and headed back to Panama City Beach.

We saw Dad right before his biopsy. Dad was still his stern order-giving self before his needle biopsy which brought us all comfort. He requested a visit from Father Kaminski. The priest from the local Catholic church came and gave Dad spiritual preparation for death, his last confession, and his last rites. Just in case he passed away during the biopsy procedure.

Jim, Mom, and I were asked to leave the room when Father Kaminski arrived. Confession and last rites happened behind closed doors.

We shuffled back to Dad's room when Father Kaminski left. Dad seemed at peace. But then he looked over at my mother and barked, "Mary, if I die, do not get messed up with the church."

In my head, I was thinking that my dad might need to confess again. Out loud, I said, "Thank you for being my dad."

My mom then barked at me, "Don't say that. You're jinxing him right before surgery."

My dad looked at me and ordered, "Take care of your mother."

I teared up and said, "I will try."

Jim and I headed toward the door to leave. We were out the door, but Jim backstepped into the room. He looked at my father and said, "Thank you for being her dad."

My dad survived the biopsy, but he died shortly after the subsequent
surgery to remove the tumor. My brother Chris was with him.
Farris Moore Elgee was born October 10, 1937 in Skowhegan, Maine.
He passed away Saturday, January 15, 2011.

146

Dad wore Old Spice cologne—old school from the white bottle. A splash
here, a splash there. Months after Dad died, my mom gave Jim a case of
unused Old Spice cologne from Dad's bathroom vanity.

Not a circle of life moment. We gifted the Old Spice cologne to
Goodwill. I do wear men's Old Spice antiperspirant. Shower Fresh scent.
Weird. I own it. Jim knows.

147

The Middle School Director position became available at my school.
I applied. Not an easy process. Public speeches followed by Q&A,
interviews with various constituencies, and social mingling. Mingling
was the toughest.

I had strong competition: an incredibly competent candidate with a PhD.
I was fairly certain my Head of School preferred the PhD candidate.
Interviews and visits ended in December. Then, radio silence. No news
for four months. I thought the wait cruel. Finally, in April, I was offered
the director position.

The salary offered was lower than what I was making as a teacher
supplemented by what I was making as a Special Lecturer. We had two
daughters in college. I could not take a pay cut. I negotiated the proposed
offer to match my current earnings. I rationalized that one job was better
than having two jobs. My counteroffer was accepted.

The new position was challenging. A good challenge. I loved it.

148

About a year later, I applied to Vanderbilt University. I wanted to complete a master's degree in education, with an independent school leadership focus. My degrees were in English, not education. I was accepted and enrolled.

I had to be on the Vanderbilt campus for seven weeks for the next two summers. Olivia helped with Teddy during my absence, driving him to summer camp, taking him on long bike rides after camp, drawing pages and pages of imagined creatures together, and going to the neighborhood pool.

I drove the ten hours from Detroit to Nashville, telling myself I would use the seven weeks away from home to learn and to get in shape. My first morning on campus, I hit the pavement. I hadn't gone running in three years, so I was pleased to have geographic anonymity. After running three blocks—sweating and heaving—I heard a loud "Collleeeen!" I kept running. Again, "Colleeeeen!!!" I turned around. There, jogging to catch up with me, was a student I had in 6th and 7th grade English, about nine years previous. He was now pre-med at Vanderbilt.

The second summer of Vanderbilt was eye-opening. During a module on Finance, I sat by Steve. He whispered to me, "Do you know about GuideStar?"

"No," I said, "what is it?"

"A platform to look up the financials of a school, including the salaries of anyone making above $100,000." Steve went on to show me how to log-in and search for my school.

What I saw shocked me. A school colleague, my colleague, who worked the same position that I worked was making much more than I. During the next class break, I called my Head of School. I probably should have waited. I was emotional.

I said to my boss, "I just learned about GuideStar today. I have never felt more like a patsy in my life."

"Colleen, external candidates take more money to attract."

My dad would have told him, "Bullshit."

I told him, "Good-bye" and returned to class. That day, something inside me broke.

149

It was not the amount of money I was earning; it was the pay disparity. The hurt ran deep.

As Teddy entered his fifth-grade year, I began looking for a new Head of Middle School position. A recruiter sent my paperwork to a school in Florida. I had flip-flopped between Michigan and Florida more than once, so the location was interesting: closer to my mother and no state income taxes. The school program seemed strong, and two University of Michigan graduates were on the Board of Trustees.

I was invited for a school visit to interview with various constituencies, to tour the campus, and to meet with HR. The HR Director informed me that faculty and staff children pay a set cost each year. Teddy's school tuition would be thousands of dollars less expensive. During the campus tour, otters were playing in a wetland area on campus. It is hard not to want to work alongside otters. The Head of School reminded me of colleague Emery—someone I could learn from. Someone who would push me. I left wanting a job offer.

The next day, I received an offer. It was a good offer: salary and moving allowance. Jim and I discussed the employment shift. He would have to take early retirement. He was eligible. We would live just a couple of hours from the Florida Keys—our most visited vacation spot. Jane lived in Florida. Chris lived in Florida. Mom lived in Florida. Downside: We would be far from all five daughters. We rationalized that they were not necessarily going to stay geographically fixed. Michigan rooted. They were all adults now. Capable of flight.

My dad coached me never to accept the first offer as is. Always negotiate. I called the Head of School and thanked him for the offer. I said everything looked good on the Offer of Employment; however, I would need $3,000 more in annual salary to accept the position.

He responded, "Of course."

Ted and I moved to Florida the following July. Jim followed in September. He had to stay back to manage the closing of the house.

150

A girlfriend of mine said, "You need to say good-bye to Carla. It is cruel to keep her alive like this. You cannot take her to Florida." Carla, who was still our stoic, beloved cattle dog, was old, deaf, and seizure prone. With mobility issues. The Carla good-bye was hard.

After emotions settled, Jim politely sighed, "We have had 16 years with dogs. Now, we can have 16 years without dogs." Seemed a reasonable statement. At the time.

151

Our five daughters, who are now independent adults, now have adult conversations. Sometimes about Jim and me.

They have a theory based on a small sample set (three homes) that no matter where Jim and I live on planet Earth we will purchase the smallest house on the largest lot. Not a California ranch, not a split-level ranch, not a storybook ranch. No split bedroom plan. The most basic ranch. Minimal bathrooms. One, ideal. Bedrooms located off an extremely narrow hallway.

When we moved to Florida we purchased the third house of our marriage. Our daughter Sophie came to visit, she said, "Mom, it's the same house." I did push back a little. I said the yard is different. No sycamore, no red maples, no snapdragons, no jack-in-the-pulpits. Climate incompatible.

At first, our new house had little tree variety: roughly sixty palm trees and one cypress tree. I loved the cypress tree. Jim added over 100 trees. I did not know the Latin names of any of the plants or trees in our backyard. Jim knew them all. We had a thick hammock of banana-type trees, including plantains. There was a sizeable orchard of fruit trees, from Meyer lemon to kumquat, from key lime to sapodilla, from guava to longan, from guanabana to moringa. The moringa is not fruit-centric; the leaves are eaten.

Two bougainvillea plants were planted with the expectation of thick leaves and bountiful blooms. Not so much. After planting, both our bougainvillea lost all their leaves and blooms, but they limped back to life. We learned, in Florida, dead-looking plants are often not dead. Just dormant. Resting. "Pining for the fjords."

At Lowe's, Jim found a broken orchid plant in a bargain bin in the back of the store for a dollar. He bought it and stuck it in a fold of a tree in the backyard. Jim drove to FruitScapes Nursery in Bokeelia, Florida and picked up two trees: a cashew tree and a macadamia tree. He told me the nursery had this sign out front: "The best time to plant a tree is twenty years ago. The second-best time is now." I liked that sentiment.

152

I stole a floor lamp. Just months before I moved to Florida, my sister Jennifer and brother-in-law Scott gifted me some beautiful furniture. They bought a new house in Ann Arbor, Michigan and decided to go with a modern décor. I booked a mover to pick up her unwanted pieces and put them in storage. Scott was there to supervise the furniture pick-up. He tagged a floor lamp as mine, so the movers took it to my rented 10x20 storage unit.

A week later, Jim and I added our household furniture to the storage unit in preparation for our impending move, planning to move our belongings down after we closed on a house. About two months after we arrived in Florida, my sister called me to explain that Scott accidentally gave me a floor lamp that was supposed to stay with them. I told Jennifer that the lamp was, at the current moment, unreachable, buried behind all our household furniture in the Michigan storage unit. I promised Jennifer that when we moved our furniture out of the storage unit, I would get her lamp back to her. In my defense, family promises have more bend than regular promises.

I ended up asking my daughter Sarah to meet the moving truck at our Michigan storage unit. Jim, Teddy, and I were already in Naples. My new job started. Sarah agreed to supervise the loading of the truck that would take our household belongings to Florida.

I hated asking Sarah to take a morning off work to do this. I hate asking for help. Ever. That said, I will ask Sarah for help. Sarah was a full-of-energy child. At two years of age, every evening, Sarah would slap her own face to avoid falling asleep. This lasted for hours until she finally succumbed to her tiredness. During her elementary years, Sarah once ran off the soccer field in the middle of a championship game to hide in the bushes after missing a goal. It took me quite a while to cajole her out of the tangled, mass of shrubbery. At sixteen, Sarah totaled her car in the snow twenty minutes after I told her not to drive in the snow. My lack of parenting experience and Sarah's natural stubborn streak were quite the combination. We both owe each other—in a good way.

I was so thankful to Sarah for meeting the moving truck. One enormous moving favor was enough. I could not bring myself to give Sarah a second task: To snag Jennifer's heavy floor lamp from our belongings and to drive it to Ann Arbor to Jennifer.

Wasn't going to happen. Instead, the floor lamp, loaded on the moving truck, traveled 1,138 miles from its rightful owner. To Florida. Returned to Jennifer seven years later. Promise kept.

153

I tackled a lengthy book that I was gifted, titled *Deep River* by Karl Marlantes, 717 pages. A big investment of time, but it was time well spent. A saga about a Finnish family—dysfunction, love, tragedy, and triumph. And a happy ending. I like happily ever after.

My enduring takeaway from *Deep River*, however, is a single word: *sisu*. *Sisu*, a Finnish word with no direct English translation, roughly meaning "white-knuckled courage" or "stoic determination and grit" or "extraordinary determination in the face of extreme adversity" as held by the Finns, integral to Finnish culture.

I have not yet experienced extreme adversity, but I am glad to know that *sisu* exists as a word and as a human capacity.

154

The Naples school proved immediately wonderful for me—but tougher for Teddy.

My colleagues were expert teachers. I had the privilege of observing artist and art teacher Mr. Geyer during the first week of school.

Mr. Geyer was teaching 6th grade students how to build a perpetual compass to use as a drawing tool for an intricate art project. What Mr. Geyer was asking students to do was insanely hard, requiring complex math, exacting measurement, and meticulous execution. Mr. Geyer was leading students towards frustration and error. The students, however, were ecstatic, leaning forward on stools, asking questions, some even requesting if they could modify the assignment, upping the difficulty level of an already difficult venture.

Mr. Geyer was fearless. The students were fearless. Even though the next few art classes promised the active use of erasers and a scrap heap of flawed beginnings, the mistakes were packaged as part of the adventure. Insanity started to look beautiful. The crazy person in me wanted to interrupt the class and tell Mr. Geyer's students that today in art class they had discovered the secret of life (or at very least a sane approach to living): dream big, expect mistakes, enjoy both. I stayed quiet. Pointing out the profundity of a moment in the moment tends to ruin the profundity of the moment.

My new colleagues were dedicated professionals. Bonus: One colleague played bagpipes. Mr. Lindner. He played the bagpipes during morning carline twice a year: on Robert Burns's birthday and on the final Friday of classes each school year. His playing touched me every time. A selfless gift. Unpaid. Relational, not transactional.

Bagpipes have an arresting sound—the music always seems just about to go off the rails but manages instead an intriguing complexity of song.

I imagine that the same folks who don't care for bagpipes, are the same folks who ask, "How can you work in middle school?" They just don't get it.

Teddy being Teddy did not like change. But he rallied every day for seven years—his highlights included finding a core group of friends, joining Scuba Gang with Jim, volunteering to do maintenance on a horse farm, and connecting with teachers and curriculum. Music was a constant as well—maybe a lifesaver. King Gizzard and the Lizard Wizard. Chicano Batman. Saxophone. Voice. Piano. Teddy absolutely hated the May-September Florida weather. Hot. He loved Michigan.

155

When a middle school student does not follow published locker rules, Mr. Kirk tapes an 8.5 x 11 notice on the student's locker that reads, in bolded, all-caps, "LOCKER VIOLATION."

Teddy received his first locker violation before Thanksgiving Break. When I asked Teddy about it, he explained that he does not keep his locker locked because doing so requires him to have to remember the combination, then to unlock the lock, and then to get his books all within the 5-minute time window between classes. Teddy explained that felt too stressful.

I counter-explained that the need to perform under pressure is a necessary life skill, and he needs to practice managing rushed situations—as well as to follow school rules.

Teddy left the LOCKER VIOLATION notice taped to his locker for weeks. "Oh no," I thought, "a rebel with a cause." Because I am an experienced mother, I did not immediately confront Teddy. I waited a few days. On a drive into school one morning, I causally asked, "Why is the LOCKER VIOLATION notice still on your locker?"

"I left it there."

"Why don't you take it down?"

Teddy deadpanned with compliant revenge, "It may be the only award I ever receive."

156

I messed up. Nothing too big. I texted my daughter Olivia birthday greetings and sent an e-gift card. I was relieved to have remembered. I am not the best when it comes to calendars, scrapbooks, and phone calls. Later that afternoon, Olivia texted in reply. "A couple days early, but THANK YOU!!!"

Drat. In my defense, October is a particularly birthday-aggressive time: sister Jane, October 2; daughter Olivia, October 7; husband Jim, October 9. My dad, October 10. Perhaps the collective pheromones from all October birthdays prompted my birthday misstep with Olivia. I am rarely early. Strange. Birthday-wise, daughter-wise, the latest I have ever been is two weeks. Apologies to Sophie.

My sister Jennifer has a sane June birthday, not October. And Jennifer, who loves birthdays, calls June her "birthday month." Yes—she celebrates and expects to be celebrated for the entire month. She started this birthday inflation in young adulthood.

I used to think it slightly bold that Jennifer parlayed 30-days of birthday out of a 1-day event. Over the years, my sister Jane and I have rolled our eyes more than once during Jennifer's month. Over time though, Jane and I have happily borrowed Jennifer's birthday month model.

157

On a drive into school, I found myself abruptly asking Teddy to repeat after me, "Mom, you do not have to worry about my schoolwork."

I told Teddy if he could say these words to me, I could relax for the day. He looked at me like I was senseless. He started to argue that reciting a few words on command doesn't mean anything.

I interrupted, "No arguing. No meaning. Just say the words. I just need to hear the words." Teddy leaned into the game. He is good like that.

Teddy recited in a slightly mocking tone, "Mom, you do not have to worry about my schoolwork." I sighed an exaggerated sigh of relief. He laughed. I smile.

Good parenting? No. In my defense, parenting often feels like the ultimate sink or swim challenge. Sometimes I wallow at the bottom of the pool.

158

For many years, holiday travel was the holiday tradition—no gifts, no tree. Our time together was the gift. Things have changed.

Now, Sarah, Sophie, Olivia, Marne, and Corrine are adults, living far away. Jobs, opinions, college, boyfriends, husbands, in-laws, children, and pets. No failure to launch scenarios. Our daughters live full lives apart from us. Celebrate holidays apart from us. Isn't that the end game of parenting? Hamlet whispers in my ear, "Ay, there's the rub."

When we vacationed as a family at Christmas, I was liberated from holiday gift-giving. A good thing because I am not so good at gift-giving.

The girls know I am challenged. I try too hard, or I give up and default to gift cards or cash.

Once I had a brilliant idea. I purchased five Vera Bradley tote bags, large size. On Black Friday. Online. On sale. I rationalized: The girls now have adult lives. They need adult-sized tote bags. It was fun picking out five different color schemes and five different patterns. Jane would be appalled by my pattern choices. She condemned paisley about ten years ago. Vera Bradley lives and breathes paisley. I like paisley. I may even really like paisley.

A week later, the Vera Bradley tote bags arrived in the mail. I was not satisfied with my purchase. Four of the five tote-bags looked beautiful. One tote was unattractive. I would say ugly, but the word feels too mean. The only task I hate worse than shopping is returns, so I thought the situation through. I am not good with fashion decisions—just ask Jane. So quite possibly there are actually four unattractive totes and one attractive tote. I am not qualified to judge. Solution: I wrapped all five totes individually. Scrambled the packages. I mailed a tote to each daughter. Pattern-blind. Color-blind.

I ended up sending each daughter an e-gift card as a supplementary gift worried that my tote idea was lame, but not quite as lame as the embroidered tree ornaments of U.S. Presidents that I once gifted sent to Grayson, Jillian, and Jack, three of my grandchildren. The ornaments have become sort of nostalgia-cool with each passing year. Sort of.

159

My older sister Jennifer texted me the following message on New Year's Eve: "Happy New Year."

The text instantly felt off. It felt cold—as if my sister was electronically reminding me of her superiority: first daughter trumps third daughter;

5 feet, 8 inches outdoes 5 feet, 7.5 inches; federal judge beats middle school principal.

Why not "Happy New Year!" with a warm, accepting exclamation point? The lingering baggage of our childhood came with that period.

Am I crazy? No, typical. Electronic communication, whether a cellphone text or social media, leaves the reader vulnerable to misinterpreting or over-reading the message due to the lack of an in-person context. And periods are a tricky—delivering a slap in the face or heavy finality. Periods never feel light by text. To me.

I love my sister Jennifer, and we get along well. She could tone down the overachieving a bit, but I'll get over it. And I do not as a habit misread tone or meaning, but it happens. Ask Jim.

160

My granddaughter Stella Josephine is named after her grandfather Joseph Patrick.

Teddy and Stella have a wonderful relationship. Every time Uncle Teddy visits, Stella greets him with the same words spoken broadcaster-loud: "Teddy, you're a human!" Stella and her sister Mary Colleen then dissolve into giggles. They have been doing this for years. The joke never gets old.

I have achieved a bit of infamy in my relationship with Stella. Remember when Will Smith slapped comedian Chris Rock at the Oscars? Slapgate 2022.

Well, when Stella was almost 5 years old and engaged in an all-out physical brawl with her sister Mary, I intervened and unthinkingly spanked Stella. Stella howled in anger. I immediately texted my daughter Sophie to confess: "I spanked Stella."

For the record, I have raised six children, and I can count on one hand the number of physical corrections given. And these were more swats than spanks. I am not a spanking-prone person. I have six grandchildren: Grayson, Jillian, Jack, Mary, Stella, and Oscar. I am guilty of spanking one grandchild, one time. Stella. Spankgate. I did it. Guilty. Remorseful. Humbled. Stella has since forgiven me. But not forgotten.

When I see Stella, she sits next to me on the couch and affectionately reminisces, "Remember when you spanked me." And I respond, "Stella, I am human." And she snuggles nearer to me.

161

After school, Teddy plopped himself into the car. We began pulling out of the school parking lot.

I asked, "How was your day?"

"Okay," he responds.

"It might be good to talk it through with me."

"I like to think things through by myself."

"Please."

"Okay. I am not sure that when I think about myself that I think about myself as I actually am or if I think about myself as perceived by me which is, therefore, not my actual self."

"Do you know the difference between the term interpersonal skills and the term intrapersonal skills?"

"Yes."

Undaunted by his knowledge, I plowed on, "Interpersonal skills are the skills you use in dealing with other people. How well do you interact with others? What is the quality of your relationships with others? Intrapersonal skills are the skills you use in dealing with yourself. How well do you interact with yourself? Know yourself? What is the quality of the relationship you have with yourself?"

"Okay."

"If you do not know how wonderful you are and love yourself as much as I love you, as much as your dad loves you, and as much as your sisters love you, then we need to have an intervention."

"Mom, I think you mean that I need an intravention. You know—to discuss my relationship with myself."

"Okay."

162

This morning, I poured myself some Wheat Chex, cut up a banana, and added milk. I then opened the silverware drawer. No spoons. We have eight spoons in our three-person household. I am not sure the ideal ratio between household inhabitants and number of spoons owned, but an 8:3 ratio is not it. I washed a spoon. I finished my cereal and placed the used bowl and spoon in the sink. Re-establishing the status quo.

I may have felt a buried twinge of pity for the next spoon-needing Potocki. But it was buried deep. I certainly would have felt empathy if I had thought to feel it. A well of compassion did not bubble up. Compassion requires action, the urge to eliminate hardship. Is spoon washing a hardship? My subconscious self obviously said, "No." In short, I did not wash the sink of dishes. I sat down to work instead.

I am certain Jim would have done all the dishes in that moment, driven by his want of order and cleanliness. He is wired like that. Not Teddy. I am certain Teddy, demonstrating a maturity beyond his years, would have simply adjusted his breakfast decision based on eating utensil availability. In the case of spoonlessness, Teddy would abandon cereal and make toast.

163

I played *Words with Friends* with my sister Jennifer. For many years. The game is a cell phone version of *Scrabble*. We played through the Covid years. Play therapy.

Every time a game ends, Jennifer begins another with me. When we first started playing, Jennifer routinely beat me. No surprise. She played with her colleagues and friends for years. I was a rookie. But I started catching up. On May 17, 2020, I won a nail-biter. Final score: 378-372. Then came what I call the turnaround game. On May 30, 2020, I was on fire. I played the word "hounding" for 111 points. I won the match: 564 points to 365 points. The student has become the master.

Okay, not really. Jennifer and I are pretty much equal in *Words with Friends* skill. We fell into a roughly 50-50 split when it came to wins and losses. Why or how do I know the dates of all my wins? In true younger sister form, I saved a screenshot of my every win. Once Jennifer beat me in an excruciatingly close game, my sibling immaturity surfaced. For revenge, I texted her—at 5 second intervals, one-at-a-time, a scoreboard screenshot of each game I had ever won.

Teddy and I found this adolescent retaliation uproariously funny. We laughed until we cried, imagining Jennifer receiving the text ambush of my former moments of superiority. On Jennifer's end, silence. And then more silence. The silence eventually became uncomfortable. My guilt set in. I put a psychological win in the Jennifer column.

I texted, "I'm sorry." Instead of responding directly, Jennifer simply started a new *Word with Friends* game with me.

164

Our daughter Marne came to visit. For the summer, Marne was going to work at a camp in Wisconsin—Camp Interlaken—as the social-emotional counselor for campers grade 3 through grade 10. Camp Interlaken is lucky to have her.

Marne visited Florida for just four days. With the busy end of the school year, I had just one full day to spend with her. We had time for a quick trip to Waterside Shops. I do not much care for shopping, but I rarely get to give Marne anything. She will lend anyone anything, but she takes very little. Marne let me spoil her with a pair of Lululemon leggings. And a pair of pajama shorts from Free People. Both for Camp Interlaken. Then, we ran over to West Marine for some practical camping shorts. Columbia. A transactional approach to love and caring—I tend to lean this direction. I come by it honestly. And the love is there.

That evening, Marne and I watched a new series together. We happened upon *Bridgerton*—a show about eight siblings looking to find love in London in 1813. After watching one episode, we were hooked. We binged three episodes that night. I joked with Marne that she was the character Eloise Bridgerton through and through. A fandom website describes Eloise as "Whip-smart, brazen, and rebellious… definitely not here for turning into just another young simpering and mincing debutante."

Teddy loved every minute with Marne. She taught him gin rummy. They binge-played. While Teddy and I were at school, Marne and Jim went to a Tiger Tail Beach for swimming and ate at The Little Bar Restaurant, splitting calamari and crab cakes.

Then, Marne left. Back to her adult life.

165

Teddy broke the screen of his recently purchased Apple laptop that we bought used. When Teddy presented me with the broken technology, he said, "The screen cracked," not "I cracked the screen." In the economic emotion of the moment, I had a hard time not placing pronoun blame.

After I calmed down, I took Teddy to Best Buy and we purchased a replacement Apple laptop. About four weeks later, Teddy came into my office and uttered three words that I thought I'd never hear again: "The screen cracked."

I barely held my calm. Two broken screens within a month's time. Okay, I was not calm. My face twitched. I said an irritated word or two, but I was quick to shift to an eerie, heavy silence.

I collected my thoughts. Material goods lack permanence. I know this.

166

Channeling the Black Knight from *Monty Python and the Holy Grail* has helped me as a parent—specifically the scene in which King Arthur and the Black Knight engage in swordplay. King Arthur cuts off the Black Knight's arm and the Black Knight says, "Tis but a scratch." King Arthur goes on to take off his other arm, then right leg, then left leg. The Black

Knight responds with quips such as "I've had worse" and "It's just a flesh wound."

As a parent, I've lived my own battles as the Black Knight. When the school nurse told me my daughter with thick, waist-length hair had lice. "Tis but a scratch." When my son had a screaming rant damning the inventor of the reset button at the annual school Bowl-a-thon in front of 200 school parents. "I've had worse." When a parent showed up on my doorstep with paper in hand to show me what my daughter posted online. "It's just a flesh wound." Defeat is not an option when parenting and a sense of humor is useful.

In *The Old Man and the Sea*, Ernest Hemingway wrote, "…man is not made for defeat. A man can be destroyed but not defeated." I love this idea—whether in Monty Python or Hemingway. I told Teddy that I wanted one gift for Christmas: for him to read Ernest Hemingway's *Old Man and the Sea* and for us to visit the Hemingway House in Key West over holiday break. Teddy replied, "Mom, that is two gifts."

It is a 4.5-hour drive to the Big Pine Key Campground where we stay over the holidays. A good time for Teddy to read. I couldn't find my paperback copy of *Old Man and the Sea*, so he listened to the novella using Audible, 2 hours, 22 minutes in length. Charlton Heston was the reader—a fact not fully appreciated by a 12-year-old. Teddy did not like listening without seeing the words in print, but he found he was able to concentrate on the audio if he put a blanket over his head. Teddy liked *The Old Man and the Sea*, but said he wished the story had ended differently for Santiago (the Old Man).

Hemingway politics is tricky. While I was standing in line to buy tickets to tour the Hemingway House, a father in front of me was telling his son that Hemingway was a drunk who killed himself. "A bit reductive," I thought. But I kept my mouth shut. He gets to parent his child. Bryan Stevenson in his book *Just Mercy*, states, "Each of us is more than the worst thing we've ever done." It's a perspective I carry with me. So Hemingway's four tumultuous marriages, dated machismo, and a variety of unsettling biographical nuggets do not negate my affection for the author. I love his writing and especially his ability to have packed so much living into one lifetime.

Teddy enjoyed touring the Hemingway House—reading the biographical placards and seeing a few 6-toed cats. As we were walking away from the Hemingway House, Teddy, happy with the experience, asked, "Do you think I can work here as a tour guide someday?" We picked up not one, but two souvenir refrigerator magnets. The magnets served as a continuous, subversive parental nudge every time Teddy opened the fridge: "Teddy, you should consider a career as a writer" or "Teddy, you should read more Hemingway." Kidding. Okay, sort of kidding.

Teddy asked me for a gift for Christmas: to go see the movie *Aquaman* at the Silverspot Theatre. The *Aquaman* movie runtime seemed eerily familiar: 2 hours, 22 minutes. Does Teddy look this stuff up to taunt me? The movie adventure ended up okay. Aquaman, half-Atlantean and half-human, battles against his half-brother Orm to unite the Kingdoms of Atlantis. Not quite Monty Python or Hemingway, but "I've had worse."

167

A family gathering. A glass of sangria. I am not a drinker, so it was enough to muddle my brain.

"Jim, I do not get it."

"The whole is greater than the sum of its parts," he repeated. "What is there to get?"

"The parts equal the sum. How is there more? There cannot be more." I think my sister-in-law jumped in and agreed with me.

Jim looked at me. Then, Jim looked at both of us, including my sister-in-law in the mix. He responded in a tone that suggested that it was not

his job to be explaining the obvious, "When the parts are together, they become something different, something more than when apart."
My brain clicked.

"I get it," I said sheepishly, remembering systems thinking. The Russell Ackoff lesson from my time at Vanderbilt. No more sangria.

168

Teddy asked me to make him a grilled cheese sandwich. I said, "No problem." I opened the refrigerator and pulled out the cheese, butter, and honey wheat bread. The bread bag clearly had only two slices left. I thought, "Oh no, Teddy will hate a grilled cheese sandwich made with the heels of the bread." When I opened the bag of bread, big surprise. The two remaining slices were not the ends. The reality hit me: Jim ate the loaf heels rather than leave them as the last two slices in the bag for the next Potocki.

For a second or two, I was profoundly touched. Then I realized the enormity of the act. This small gesture seemed ridiculously thoughtful— the kind of kindness that can be twisted into viewing unkindly because it is too kind. How many times have I left the heels of bread for the next sandwich maker? Every single time. Who am I? Obviously, now, a monster.

169

I have read two fish-themed books: *One Fish, Two Fish, Red Fish, Blue Fish* by Dr. Seuss and, predictably, *The Old Man and the Sea* by Ernest Hemingway. My engagement with fish would have ended there. Would have—but a family friend said to me the following words: "So you're not a boat person." Because I do like to be defined or labeled, I crankily replied, "I do not choose to place people into narrow groups: boat people or not boat people." It is a wonder that I have any friends.

I became a boat person because it was implied I was not a boat person. I fished with Jim and Teddy three times over holiday break. Fishing had its good points. I liked baiting the hook with messy, liquidy squid. The staining power of squid guts was quite remarkable. I liked talking to each fish as I carefully dehooked and released it. I liked that Red Grouper are stunningly ugly and beautiful at once.

Once we fished close to a bridge. Once we fished the back country. Once we went a long way out into open water to try our luck at the reef. The ocean at the reef looked like a completely different body of water— huge swells, heavy-looking water, expansive. Otherworldly.

While fishing is good, I still like dirt because it is firm and solid. I like having my two feet on the ground. I have a hard time trusting air travel either. I don't dislike it—though it feels like a gamble, flying 35,000 feet above the ground. So boat travel is a slightly edgy experience. I love fishing with Jim, but I am not a great swimmer, and I saw the movie *Jaws*. Not big worries. Shadow worries. Dirt is good. Jim and I had to buy a few loads of dirt for our backyard once. The cost was shocking.

170

Corrine came for a Florida visit, so Jim, Teddy, Corrine and I made the trek to Palmdale, Florida for the annual Hatching Festival. It lived up to its published promise: "a once in a lifetime opportunity to hatch a baby gator in the palm of your hand." We each hatched our own gator. And, when doing so, we each had that new parent giddiness as if having given birth to our own baby gator. Jim may remember the event differently.

With the $32.95 per person ticket price, a hatch-parent gets naming rights. I named my baby gator Suki Thai Stanislaus. In elementary school, Jane and I dreamed of getting a puppy and naming it Suki Thai

Stanislaus. Jim named his gator Wojtek—after a Syrian bear adopted by Polish troops during WWII. Corrine struggled to choose between two names: Tater and Potater. She ultimately decided to go with the more formal Potater. Teddy named his gator Owlbear—after a fictional creature in Dungeons and Dragons.

171

I am not sure I have ever been fun. I have fun. But I have never been the fun. Arguably an ugly word. Fun. Nothing good happens to the mouth when saying fun. Say it. "Fun." Just as the mouth begins to open up, it quickly closes. There is no fun in saying fun. A piranha of a word. Were there signs as I was growing up that I might not ever be the life of the party? I have never danced at a celebratory event without being hyper-aware that I was dancing. If I were fun, wouldn't I be so into dancing that I am not thinking about the fact that I am dancing? Never going to happen.

I have never tasted coffee. Honest. I do not like the smell. Perhaps there is a correlation between coffee and an entertaining personality? Frappuccino. Double shot Expresso. Latte. Java. The vocabulary of coffee seems to require an intrinsic festiveness of the drinker.

Some individuals seem genetically predisposed to be fun. No slight to the unfun intended. If everyone were fun, would anyone be fun? Without contrast, fun ceases to be. Unfun. Say it. "Unfun." Up-down. A seesaw of a word, but without the queasiness of rollercoasters.

172

During an middle school assembly, Mrs. Stevens told students that she had scheduled a guest speaker for assembly, but he had a last-minute conflict and could not come. Mrs. Stevens explained that she was going to do her best to tell them what his presentation would have been. Mrs. Stevens shared that Mr. Andy Casagrande, an Emmy-award winning oceanographer, was going to tell them about the sharks he had photographed all over the world.

Before Mrs. Stevens could continue, Casagrande ran out from behind the stage curtain and shouted, "Surprise! We are just kidding. I am here!" I liked his surprise entrance. Casagrande went on to give students a show-and-tell presentation about his experience photographing sharks all over the world, sharing videos of his dives in New Zealand, South Africa, Mexico, and Australia. Casagrande was captivating.

He brought props—several different types of Go-Pro cameras; a huge, expensive underwater camera to capture footage for shark movies; and his two Emmys. I went up on stage after Casagrande's talk to thank him for visiting the students. As I walked by his Emmy statues, I touched one of them. I touched an Emmy. I am oddly thrilled by that fact. Surprises are wonderful.

173

Jim and I sat on our patio breathing in the smoky air and looking at the odd reddish hue in the sky. Wildfires. I asked Jim if we'd be okay. He answered, "I've danced with the devil before," quoting a line from the movie *Backdraft*. Oddly reassuring.

174

Before his death, Dad told Mom, "Mary, just stay put." Not sure why he told Mom this, but it helped at the time. Everyone had their orders. And for nine years Mom felt comfortable and content just staying put.

I was now in Naples. Jane moved to Naples, too. Mom resided in Panama City Beach, Florida. Near Chris. Chris had been looking after Mom since Dad passed—and both of them before that.

Mom was about 8.5 hours from Naples by car. No direct flights available. Hard to get to her. Jane wanted to bring Mom to Naples to live with her. After repeated requests from Jane, Mom finally agreed to move to Naples. For our part, Jim and I volunteered to go get Mom and bring her to Naples.

Mom had not been more than a few miles from her house for many years. Publix, Target, doctor, and dentist—all within a convenient radius. Jim and I worried that we'd get to Panama City Beach and she would change her mind about moving. We joked that we might have to strap her down in the backseat. Or slip her some Tylenol PM—totally kidding, but we said it out loud. We did not know what to expect. We wondered if we'd have to stop one or two or three nights on the journey back to Naples, not knowing if Mom had the stamina for a lengthy road trip.

Mom was a dream. She packed two large boxes of belongings—one with clothes, one with paperwork and keepsakes. Mom wanted nothing else loaded into the pickup truck. At eighty-one years old, her only demand was that we dine exclusively at Panera Bread restaurants on our travel back to Naples. Fair enough.

Mom loved the adventure of journeying to Naples and preferred to make the whole trip in one day. Jennifer and Jane surreptitiously texted me during the long drive asking for updates. I kept disappointing them with "She's fine"—for which they were glad, but they had anticipated a little family drama.

After we stopped at Panera Bread for breakfast, Mom quipped, "I wonder where the next Panera will be." Jim scouted the next convenient Panera, making four Panera stops enroute back to Naples. Mom was content. Jim was a saint.

Mom lived happily in Naples with my sister Jane. Jane spoiled my mom. And I was spoiled with Mom's proximity. I visited every weekend, often with Teddy. Mom gave Teddy a $20 bill each time he visited her. He politely refused. She insisted. When considering a purchase, Teddy joked, "I'd have to visit Nana ten times to afford that."

175

At some juncture, on every given morning, I ask myself, "Where are my car keys?" If Jim is awake, he responds, "Where you left them." Sometimes the keys are in my purse, sometimes in the mail basket by the side door, sometimes on the small table by the front door, sometimes they are on the black recliner in the bedroom, sometimes they are in my book bag, sometimes they are on the kitchen counter, and sometimes they are on the dining room table. Ninety-seven percent of the time I find my keys in one of these places. Where I left them.

Maybe I unconsciously like to go on a search mission every morning because I have a relatively good chance of finding my "lost" keys. I begin the day with an easy win. And if I fail to find my keys, I quietly sneak the spare set off of Jim's dresser. Yes, my life might be slightly easier if I put my car keys in the exact same place every time I return home. Who wants to live like that?

I like to believe every adult clings to some small sliver of youthful abandon, pushing against responsibility whether neglecting to keep an umbrella handy during rainy season or not replacing the tabs on the car license plate until expired. In our family, Uncle Mark balks at the printed expiration dates on food. He is a legend in that way. Youthful and rebellious—although now in his sixties.

At work, I am Mrs. Potocki, a person who needs to act grown up. I am mostly successful. When I get to my office, I toss my car keys in my top right desk drawer. Without fail. Except once. Every day when I leave,

I open the desk drawer and the keys are there. No drama. Very mature. Maturity is maturity. The word sounds heavy. Like manure.

176

I have a bad track record when booking accommodations for family gatherings. Once, I booked a place in Ann Arbor that was behind a liquor store and backed up to an alley for Jim, Ted, me, and Sophie's family whose children, at the time, were 3 years old and 4 years old. The large family room window in the rental was one-way glass, allowing us to look out but not allowing outsiders to look in. The alley traffic was active—foot traffic peaking at about 2:00 a.m. A little unsettling seeing dark figures walking inches from our rental window in the dead of night. But this was not my scariest rental pick.

Jim, Teddy, and I planned to stop in Savannah for two days to break up a road trip from Florida to Michigan. I booked a modest, historic home in downtown Savannah. All was well with our lodgings, except that the bathroom was undergoing a remodel. A sizeable hole occupied the bathroom ceiling. More hole than ceiling surface.

Savannah is often called "America's Most Haunted City." I am a pragmatic person, but I must admit Savannah felt haunted. It was hard to think of a hole in the bathroom ceiling as merely remodeling-in-progress. Heck no—it was a ghost hole. A hole of paranormal activity. To exacerbate the situation, Jim, Teddy, and I went on a night-time ghost tour on the first evening of our two-night stay. After that, it was hard for me to feel even moderately composed when using the rental restroom. The *Psycho* shower scene came to mind more than once. I went back-and-forth about whether it was better to keep my eyes on the gaping hole or whether it was better to avoid looking at it. I ultimately decided not only to avoid looking at the hole but also to say the ABCs in my head over-and-over to keep my mind occupied.

177

One school morning, Teddy had a headache. As we drove into school, Teddy slumped in the passenger seat.

I asked, "How are you feeling, Teddy?"

He replied, "I feel miserable."

Momentary pause. Then, I went off the rails. "Teddy, you can choose to be miserable, or you can choose to be something more than miserable, like 'I feel miserable, but I am going to pull myself through it.' If you stop at the word *miserable*, you are wallowing. Adding something positive after the word *miserable* will help you move away from the misery."

Teddy just looked at me. Miserable.

178

I went to pick up a prescription for my mother. Before the clerk would hand over the stapled white bag, she asked me my mother's birth date.

Over the years, when asked the date of my mother's birthday, I responded, "February 1st or 2nd—whichever day is not Groundhog Day." As I said this to the CVS clerk, it felt shameful. The clerk seemed unconcerned and continued questioning: "Year?" I had no ready answer. I know my mother's age, so I tried to quickly do the math in my head. The pressure was too much. I responded, "Earlyish 20th century."

I wanted to defend my ignorance by sharing memorized facts that I did know. Einsteinium is a synthetic element, symbol Es, atomic number 99. The capital of Nebraska is Lincoln. The drummer before Ringo Starr was

Pete Best. Instead, I recited my mother's home address and produced her insurance card and my driver's license. I left CVS with the prescription and a bag of daughter guilt.

I willfully refuse to file my mother's birth date in my brain. Not traveling down that road of psychoanalysis.

179

Jennifer enrolled in a Yale online class titled the Science of Well Being—a free 19-hour course described as "a series of challenges designed to increase your own happiness and build more productive habits" and as "the most popular course in the more than three-century history of Yale." Jennifer loved the course. I am curious to know if the Science of Well Being includes dog ownership. I hope Jim relents about doglessness at about year 10, not year 16.

180

Whether assigned reading or recreational reading, I try to cement in my mind an idea or words from each book read—something helpful to takeaway for further consideration or later reference. *In Thrive Through the Five*, author Dr. Siler quotes author David Weinberger. Weinberger's words now rattle about in my brain: "The smartest person in the room is the room."

I like to think about this idea. I love it. It challenges me to get out of my own head and appreciate the collective brainpower of any group meeting. Admittedly, I do like to contrast this quotation to a post I once read about committee work—meant to be read in a cynical, skeptical, Orwellian tone: "When possible, refer all matters to committees, for 'further study and consideration.' Attempt to make the committees as large as possible — never less than five." The potential of a group can derail into purposelessness and impotence.

181

Teddy celebrated his birthday a month early, because we were with family in Michigan in July. During the birthday celebration, our daughter's boyfriend Nate asked Jim if he could have our daughter Olivia's hand in marriage. Jim said, "Yes, fine with me," adding something along the lines of "Olivia does not need his approval. Olivia makes her own decisions."

Olivia loves Nate. Nate loves Olivia. We love Nate. He is family. Already. That said, I didn't realize that I had expectations about when the proposal should occur, now that Nate talked to Jim. Within 30 days. My unfettered assumption. Firmly, inexplicably rooted in my mind.

August rolled around. No proposal. September. No proposal. I found myself thinking "What the heck, Nate?" October. No proposal. "Come on, Nate. Olivia's birthday was October 7—you missed a perfect opportunity." November. No proposal. "Nate, holiday season is proposal season." December. No proposal. "Why ask permission if you are not going to propose?" January. No proposal. "This is ridiculous." February. No proposal. "Nate, are you kidding me. Why not Valentine's Day?"

I had turned into a nag of an eventual mother-in-law. Nate was rightfully living his timeline. Not my timeline for him. Good thing I kept I kept my impatient thoughts in my head.

March. Nate proposed. In St. Louis. Under the Gateway Arch.

182

My older sister Jennifer has a cabin up north in Michigan. Over the years, Jennifer has always allowed my family unfettered usage of her vacation home. It has been a place of large family gatherings and a place of quiet refuge. The cabin is very cabin-ish. Woods. Water. Comfort. Jennifer is good at making spaces feel welcoming, from furnishings to refrigerator magnets, from artwork to throw blankets. A huge, brown faux fur bear throw blanket sits draped over one of the couches. It has weight and warmth. There have been fights over who has dibs on the faux fur bear throw.

When Jane moved near me in Florida , she dropped off items to my house that would not fit in or did not match her new house. I do not say "no" to either of my sisters. My husband Jim watched, near silently, as we gained a few more possessions. For Jim, the word "possessions" is synonymous with the word "clutter." Jane gifted us a large rug, a chair, a matching ottoman, and a naked painting of our mother. My mother sat for the painting in the early 1970s. Very much a thing of the times. The portrait might actually be quite beautiful but none of us can get beyond the that's-my-mother awkwardness of it. Over the years, we have respectfully passed the mom portrait among us. I am not sure of its present location, but maybe in Chris's garage.

Jane also dropped off a grey faux fur throw blanket. Of indeterminate faux animal origin. Maybe a faux grey wolf. Maybe a pack of twenty faux grey rabbits. Very soft. I was, at first, quietly thrilled to have my own faux fur throw. It is, however, not bear-sized. It is about three quarters the size I need. A reoccurring theme with hand-me-downs.

183

It was my birthday. My daughter Sophie texted me two words: double
nickel. As is often the case when communicating with Sophie, I didn't
get it. I asked Jim. He knew. Double nickel = 55. I looked it up the
definition to confirm. Oxford English Dictionary and Urban Dictionary. I
trust Jim— but Jim and Sophie have been known to play tricks on me.

184

My son Teddy and I went to a Fall gathering. Teddy ask-demanded that
I play cornhole with him. I accepted. Our host had a lighted corn hole
arena. Very cool. But I am not captivated by glittering lights or any logo-
fueled cornhole experience. It is the bean bag of the game that gets me.
The feel of it.

Bean bags are an invention worthy of attention. *Invention* may be too
big a word—but deserved. The tactile gratification of a bean bag is huge,
but under-celebrated. In contrast, for example, clay therapy is embraced.
Readily accepted. Trendy. Swayze-Moore endorsed. My daughters Marne
and Corrine go to clay class to relax and to recenter. Any child who has
played with Play Doh knows that clay has power. I posit that a bean bag
has equal power. It feels weighty and solid but not too solid—gently
affectionate. Not too heavy, not too light. And without the messiness of
clay. Or human interaction. Life feels meaningful when you hold a bean
bag. Especially if you squish it just a little between your fingers. Just
a little squish though—if you squeeze too hard, the casing-on-casing
experience wrecks the tactile euphoria.

185

Jane and I sat with my mom for the last five days of her life. Jane was there nearly always. I came as much as I could—trying to hit work and home as needed. My mom, in writing, requested not to spend her last days in a hospital or hospice care facility. Home was her choice. Jane had provided a sanctuary for our mother in her last years of life. Mom loved Naples and living with Jane.

The five final days were awful and beautiful at once. It did seem Mom was at peace. Comfortable though dying. If Jane recited the Our Father, Mom would move her lips in recitation with her. We held her hand. Jane and I were there for her last breath. We called Jim to come over to determine with finality that Mom was no longer alive. Jim confirmed her death.

We then called Mom's doctor, the police, and mortuary transport. The police officer arrived first. He explained the protocol of the situation to Jim, Jane, and me. Jane indicated that she wanted to dress Mom for the trip to the funeral home. A skirt and blouse. I volunteered to help Jane. As we walked to the bedroom, I hesitated. I asked the officer if he had any disposable gloves. He did. I am not sure if I should be ashamed. Mom was gone. I felt the body in the bedroom was not her. I did not want to touch a dead body. Jane did not want gloves. Mom was Mom.

Mary Kathleen O'Neill was born February 1, 1939 on a family farm in Petersville, New Brunswick, Canada. She died in Naples, Florida on November 2, 2021.

Jim, Ted, and I drove Mom's ashes up to Panama City Beach to Santa Rosa Cemetery. We stayed with Frank. Chris made arrangements for the site attendant to ready Mom's place next to Dad. A small, informal ceremony. The morning was beautiful. Dad and Mom together again.

186

I received an orchid plant as a teacher gift more than once. Jim rescued each gifted orchid, knowing if left in my hands the plant was destined to die. Jim then planted them in our backyard. I am not sure planted is the correct term. Jim typically tucked the orchid plant firmly in a palm tree bark pocket and then tied it in place. Or he tied the plant directly to a tree without a comfy resting pocket. Or he placed the orchid in a homemade box wired to a tree.

All the orchids thrived. I liked watching the roots grow. Orchid roots are out in the open, not underground. They stretch and spread around the tree trunk like spidery varicose veins. Oddly beautiful. Pink, purple, yellow, amber, and white orchids grew around our backyard. For a time, our daughters were inundated with texts of orchid pictures whenever a new backyard bloom occurred. I loved the backyard orchids, intrigued by the tied-to-a-tree nurturing.

187

When we played *Friendly Feud* in middle school, the game required some hard thinking because adults were surveyed for answers, not students.

Students pushed back on one prompt, in particular: "Name a popular pizza topping." The first student team guessed "pepperoni," earning 24 points. The second team guessed "mushrooms," earning 16 points— along with groans of disgust and loud "yuks" from a vocal group of anti-mushroom students. Mushrooms evoke strong feelings in middle school students, pros and cons, not any inbetweeners. The third team did not answer right away. They took a few minutes to discuss whether "cheese" was a pizza topping or part of the pizza. One team member argued, "There is always cheese on pizza, so it is not a topping." But a shout across the room countered this assumption, "Not in my house—

just sauce and toppings. No cheese." The third team ended up taking a gutsy gamble and answered, "cheese," earning themselves a whopping 26 points. Cheese was the number one answer.

I do not hold a position on whether cheese is a pizza topping.

188

I love the short story "The Open Boat" by Stephen Crane. It is a story of four men struggling to survive in a lifeboat after their ship has gone down. After a couple of rough nights at sea, the men finally come within sight of shore. They all feel intoxicated with optimism. Each man clings to this belief: If I were going to be drown, why would fate have allowed me to come so far as to see the beach. Not all the men make it to the shore. Nature proves indifferent. Not coldly indifferent. Just indifferent.

I was showering. I felt a lump. I made an appointment to see my general practitioner that afternoon. She felt the lump, too.

The subsequent mammogram showed three areas that needed further investigation; next, an ultrasound was performed. After the ultrasound, I dressed and waited in the dressing room for my turn to meet the attending radiologist. I was patient and calm, but those dressing rooms are not happy places.

The radiologist greeted me with a somber sentence: "I am sorry we are meeting under these circumstances." An Eeyore of a radiologist. I would have preferred a tone of hardline science—skipping an overly optimistic or overly gloomy affect. He shared that I had a tumor that looked malignant. He told me he'd send the results back to my general practitioner who would then recommend a surgeon.

The breast surgeon was an exceptional doctor—delivered facts with confidence and energy. Problem-solving one step at a time based on the information in front of us. She recommended a lumpectomy to remove the areas of abnormality and some surrounding tissue. The lymph nodes under my left arm needed to be sampled, too. She had an opening next week. The next doctor I had to see was a plastic surgeon.

The plastic surgeon's waiting room was a confluence of two types of patients: those undergoing elective cosmetic surgery and those receiving reconstructive surgery because of accident or illness. I did not feel beautiful. For the first time since finding the lump, I cried. Quietly.

I was called in to meet the plastic surgeon. He was a dream—a family man with a nerdy love of reshaping body parts. He looked at my I've-seen-better-days breasts as a canvas. On the day of the surgery, he drew all over my chest with a marker. I ended up with better breasts because of the lifting and reshaping.

Now that we had information, Jim and I discussed how to tell the family. I decided to write an email. My communication received slight criticism, mostly because I left two sons-in-law off the group. My defense: I did not have their email addresses. Eventually, my family agreed that there is no right way to share cancer news.

I applied for time off work. I would miss the last five weeks of the school year. As a middle school principal, I felt crummy leaving at such a hectic time. Awards ceremonies, locker clean-up, exams, moving-up ceremony, and more. To that point, I prided myself on no sick days in six years. My colleagues covered for me.

189

The lumpectomy went as planned. The tumor pathology included good and bad news. Good news: No cancer in the lymph nodes. Bad news: The tumor staging indicated a need for further treatment. Chemotherapy and radiation. My oncologist called it "Baby-Chemo"—four rounds over 12 weeks, followed by 5 weeks of radiation. I would complete my chemotherapy before the start of the next school year.

Before treatments, Jim proposed a trip to the Salvador Dali Museum in St. Petersburg. A two-day trip. As it turned out, perfectly timed. A good distraction.

While completing chemotherapy, I worked. Summer hours. Chemotherapy treatments were social in structure—30 or so recliner chairs in a large room. I packed a lunch: green grapes, cut strawberries, half a peanut butter and blackberry jam sandwich. I brought a water bottle filled with ice water. And I brought a book. To be honest, I liked the ritual. It felt productive (cancer-killing), and I rarely had time to read or relax—the reclining felt self-indulgent.

The sickness felt from chemotherapy hit about 72 hours following each treatment. Artist Salvador Dali, in his late period, unintentionally captured on canvas the melty, fantastical feeling of chemotherapy side effects. My bones ached. When I was working on scheduling at my office desk, I sometimes felt as if my body were sliding to the floor even though I was not really moving. Definitely surreal.

190

I taught a college essay writing summer workshop after the first chemotherapy treatment. I had a two-week, ten-meeting class plotted on 102 PowerPoint slides. No worries.

On Slide 4, a picture of author Thomas M. Disch sat front and center. Disch wrote an engaging science fiction short story titled "Problems of Creativeness," published in 1967. The protagonist of the story, Birdee Ludd, must demonstrate distinct physical, intellectual, or creative abilities not evident on a standardized test.

The story plot mirrors the objective of college essay writing pretty much dead on. Well, close enough. In Disch's story, the stakes are different: A citizen who cannot effectively demonstrate individual distinction cannot marry and cannot have children. Spoiler alert. Birdie Ludd writes an eloquent, clever essay on the topic of creativity; however, the essay is machine graded, and the machine, who determines his future, does not pick up on the eloquence and cleverness of the essay. Birdie Ludd is subsequently denied reclassification. Denied marriage. Denied children.

Slide 4 is admittedly a bit of a downer, but it serves as a neat launch for discussion: "How does a college essay writer successfully demonstrate distinct physical, intellectual, or creative abilities in 650 words or less?"

Teddy was in the workshop. He wrote about lizards. His friend wrote about the universe. Another wrote about beginning his own business. Another, about a bonfire and friends.

191

Writing workshop done. I begged Jim and Teddy to leave me for the second round of treatment. They finally agreed to visit family in Michigan. Jim was not happy about leaving me. He said I was effectively sending him away. Maybe.

Jim graciously allowed me to be sick with space. Forever grateful. I started losing clumps of hair, so I went to a walk-in haircut factory. It felt neat to say, "Shave it all off." I started wearing a head scarf. I sent pictures from the parking lot to Jim.

Immediately following my third treatment, Jim, Ted, and I flew to Pennsylvania to take Teddy to visit college campuses: Gettysburg, Dickinson, Rochester, Syracuse, and Bard. I was poisoned and tired, but I knew the activity each day was therapeutic. We fit in a visit to Sophie and family. I gave Mary and Stella head scarves. Perhaps, strange. Forcing normalcy.

My last chemotherapy treatment happened on the first day of school.
No worries. I missed a couple of hours in the morning. That is all. The
effects of the final treatment hit me hard two days later. Friday. I was
walking through the crowded front office at school when I felt my legs
give. I sat down in the middle of the lobby. On the floor. No choice. A
colleague saw what was happening. She came over and sat down next to
me. On the floor. She said, "Pretend we are looking over papers."
She helped me to my desk after the lobby emptied.

Chemotherapy done.

192

The elephant is the star in at least one idiomatic expression: "There is an
elephant in the room." When courtesy dictates, adults are good at, as a
default, politely ignoring whatever elephant is in the room.

I felt a little like an elephant in the proverbial room when I returned
to campus at the start of a new school year without hair. Bald. Bald
as Yul Brynner—an actor, my first real celebrity crush. Bald as actor
Telly Savalas (aka as Kojak). I enjoyed Kojak's over-the-top NY cop
toughness and swagger during my teen years.

Unlike adults, students acknowledge the elephant in the room. Curious
about my baldness, a student approached me and bluntly asked, "Mrs.
Potocki, do you have cancer?" I explained that I had cancer, and the
treatments made my hair fall out, but there was no more cancer. I am
good. Just need to regain strength and grow hair. He smiled and skipped
off to class. Asked and answered.

Later that same day, as I walked to assembly, a student said to me,
"I like your head scarf." I thanked her. I am fashion-challenged, so the
compliment was welcome.

When I drove away from campus, I cried. Tears of relief.

193

I scheduled my radiation appointments during my lunch break, stretched to two hours in length.

I did better with chemotherapy than I did with radiation. The chemotherapy treatments were easy; the following days were hard. Radiation was the exact opposite: the treatments were psychologically tough; the days after, no major side effects. Just tiredness. Radiation treatments were intense. Big machinery, loud noises, isolation, voices over speakers, voices in my head, repeated bouts of breath holding, lasers. The stuff of science fiction.

Jane and I had a routine of jog-walking together every Sunday at 5:30 a.m. We mostly kept it up through my treatments. Some weeks I was shamefully slow. Jane kept me active.

After radiation, my surgeon started referring to me as a "cancer survivor." My oncologist said, "We are done with this one." The quoted odds are low that this cancer will return. Not sure. It is what it is.

I looked forward to having hair again. Jim jokingly asked me to stay bald. He enjoyed the universal kindness prompted by my headscarf—especially getting moved forward in wait lines, whether at restaurants, grocery store, or the DMV.

194

For better or worse, I gifted Teddy Apple AirPods (aka wireless headphones); he began binge-listening podcasts immediately—sampling to find one he liked. He settled on a podcast called *LORE*, a podcast of scary stories and twisted history. Advertised as true stories. Yikes.

Teddy's podcast selection is probably my fault. When Teddy was 5-years old, I bought him the infamous Alvin Schwartz's trilogy of children books: *Scary Stories to Tell in the Dark, More Scary Stories to Tell in the Dark,* and *Scary Stories 3: More Tales to Chill Your Bones.*

A particularly creepy story in the series is titled "The Green Ribbon." A girl named Jenny wears a green ribbon around her neck—never taking it off. A boy named Alfred is curious about the green ribbon. Jenny never explains to Alfred why she always wears the green ribbon. Alfred and Jenny eventually get married and grow old together. One fateful day, elderly Jenny gives ancient Alfred permission to untie her green neck ribbon. When he unties the ribbon, her head falls off. Not too scary. Even an edge of humor. But creepy enough.

There are only three official *Scary Story* books. The LORE podcast has 161 episodes. Yikes, again. Each episode is approximately 20 minutes. In total, roughly 3,220 minutes of eerie AirPod time. A fleeting few seconds of parental panic as I digested the calculation: maybe the 3,220 minutes would be better spent on something else. Prepping for the SAT. Practicing saxophone. Cleaning the house. But I trusted Teddy. I am convinced his years of playing Magic the Gathering are responsible for his verbal dexterity. Podcasts are a throwback to the radio broadcasts. Orson Welles, *The War of the Worlds* in 1938. Old school. Classic. Literary.

Jim and I went fishing, leaving Teddy and *LORE* on shore in the camper. The date: January 1st. The two days previous were too windy to fish. And it was still a little windy. We fished close in by a bridge, not expecting much. I caught the usual: a Porgy, a Yellowtail Snapper, a Mutton Snapper, and several Grunts. I dislike Grunts. They grunt. I am sure there are contexts in which a grunt is beautiful. I concluded the outing with a spectacular catch: a 25-inch Gag Grouper. My largest fish to date. A beautiful fish. My first keeper grouper—or so I thought. Timing is important when fishing. Gag Grouper season ran from June 1-December 31. I caught my big fish one day too late. His timing was impeccable.

Life after AirPods was different, the car rides into school became unusually quiet. *LORE* quiet. If I wanted to speak to Teddy, I had to physically touch him to get his attention. He then tapped his ear twice to pause his AirPods and said, "What?" An odd conversational ritual.

195

I asked Teddy to think of something we could talk about. He replied, "Jellyfish." Jellyfish. Too narrow and not something I know much about, so I then asked him to give me ten topic ideas. Teddy responded, "Atlantic Sea Nettle, Box Jellyfish, Lion's Mane Jellyfish, Cannonball Jellyfish, Purple-Striped Jellyfish, Flower Hat Jellyfish, Blue Button Jellyfish…." He was cracking himself up.

What do I find funny? The Marvelous Miss Maisel. A comedy-drama set in the late 1950's about a stand-up comedienne. Gender-specific word. Usage intentional. Time period appropriate. Jim and I binged-watched a couple of shows each night until done. When we viewed Episode 4, I gasped. A clown-comedian, known as Red Skelton, made a sudden appearance on the television screen. Jim and I looked at each other—a simultaneous rush of wonky nostalgia. Not quite pleasant but a familiar homey feel. The Red Skelton Hour was a staple in both our childhood households. We did not actually watch Red Skelton. My dad did. His dad did. Red Skelton was more a clown for adults. When my dad watched The Red Skeleton Hour, I played in the TV room with my unbendable Barbie. The Red Skelton Hour was little more than background noise. I avoided glancing at the clown-man on the television screen. Unsettling.

I am not judging any clowns or clown-lovers. Good people, I am sure. Red Skeleton is not responsible for my dislike of clowns. In the late 1960s the Bozo the Clown franchise was a big deal. I repeat. A clown franchise. Many different actors played Bozo across America. Each big city had its own Bozo. Children didn't know there were many Bozos. Children thought Bozo was Bozo. One clown. During my childhood, Detroit had three Bozo the Clowns in relatively quick succession. I noticed the unexplained changes in Bozo—his voice was squeakier, he seemed taller, and now his shoulders had an odd droop.

196

Olivia and Marne visited. Still grown-up. Olivia came from Michigan; Marne, North Carolina. On Friday, Marne landed in Punta Gorda at 10:21 a.m. Olivia landed in Fort Myers at 12:36 p.m. Jim graciously managed the two-airport pick-up. Over the weekend, we visited the South Street Farmer's Market, walked the little piece of city pier. A big chunk of the pier is still closed—hurricane damage. We walked more at the Frida Kahlo exhibition at the botanical gardens and dined at Island Gypsy Café. But mostly, we hung around the house where there was a stash of unopened games that Teddy received for Christmas. I am not sure exactly why Santa chose to give the sole remaining child in the household a slew of multi-player games, but she did.

Teddy, Marne, and Olivia played the games. They played *Jaipur*, a tactical game in which each player vies to be appointed the Maharaja's personal trader. An odd premise, but Olivia secretly told Santa to get Teddy this game. Good advice. Next, they played the card game *Peace*, a card game played like the card game War, but players win with kindness. The "I made you dinner" card is worth 5 points; the "I painted your house" card is worth 10 points. The "I washed your car" card is worth 8 points; the "I threw you a parade card" is worth 12 points. The "I helped you move" card is only worth 9 points. Gravely under-pointed. Next, they played *EXIT: The Game*, "The Abandoned Cabin" edition, an escape room structured game. Players solve puzzles to escape a locked cabin, except there isn't a locked cabin. Players have to imagine that they are in the locked cabin. In short, it is an escape room game without an actual escape room. What was Santa thinking?

On Saturday, I announced I was going to Barnes and Noble to pick up the book *The Three-Body Problem*, by Ken Lui, a book recommended by Olivia. Marne asked me to pick up the game *Everdell* and a deck of tarot cards. Barnes and Noble had all three items in stock. Before Marne conducted tarot readings on her siblings, I told-lectured Teddy fortune-telling is not real—a grifter's game. Teddy said, in his very Teddy way, "I know, Mom." Marne did a tarot reading on Teddy; then, Olivia. Marne's readings felt eerily apt. Real.

The remainder of the evening the three of them played *Everdell*—after assembling the elaborate cardboard Ever Tree, of course. The game also includes 30 berries, 20 tokens, 30 twigs, 20 pebbles, 24 wooden creatures and more. The object of the game is to construct dwellings for critters. And the player who successfully attracts the most critters wins. *Everdell* was played twice on Saturday night and again Sunday.

While the allure of *Everdell* escapes me, the house felt full. Olivia and Marne shared a queen bed in the guest room and giggled themselves to sleep each night, much like when they were in middle school.

On Monday, Jim made the two-airport run once more.

197

Jim is the youngest child in his family. I am the third of four. The unofficial loco parentis defaulted to older siblings never seems to go away. Older siblings often act like additional parents, not siblings. It has taken time, but both Jim and I have begun to be recognized as equals by our siblings. Sometimes. Recently, my oldest sister Jennifer asked me for advice. Parenting advice. First time ever. I was giddy. Jim told me to calm down.

Jim recently went fishing with his two brothers and one brother-in-law. I texted Jim during the trip to ask how things were going. He replied, "The boys are being fairly easy to get along with. I think everyone is feeling their collective mortality." Jim's words were not dark, just reality. We are getting older. As we all get older, Jim and I do not mind being the youngest siblings any longer. The need for sibling equality wanes. Enjoying the time together is primary.

On a ride into school, I asked Teddy, "Which is most important: remembering the past, living in the present, or looking forward to the future?"

Teddy responded, "*This* is what you think about?"

I replied, "Yes."

198

Jane texted me that she was getting rid of a leather loveseat. She asked, "Do you want it?" For a good long time, Jim and I had many children and a dog or two in the house. It was wiser to acquire furniture than purchase furniture. It made parenting easier.

"Yes, you can build a fort using the sectional we acquired from Jim's brother's dental practice. Of course, you can stack the pieces to make a second floor."

"Yes, you can make buttery popcorn and watch a movie on the couch passed to us from Jennifer."

"Yes, go ahead and construct a school project on the coffee table, rehomed by Jim's other brother. Use permanent marker. Do you need the glue gun, too? But no glitter. Glitter was banned."

Jim and I now had one child and no dog at home, but the extended family norm was still to offer up any unwanted furniture to us. And Jim and I still took it in.

Jim and I introduced Jane's leather loveseat into the furniture mix. Dumb. We messed up the composition of the room. We placed the loveseat off to the side under a framed 2016 French Quarter Festival poster. Designating the loveseat secondary seating, not front and center. Not a television watching couch. Problem: The loveseat looks more commanding than anything else in the room. High rolled arms and no wear and tear. I do not spend much time thinking about furniture and focal points. But the loveseat does. It whispers, "Look at me. Look at me. Look at me."

Eventually the room will feel right again. The whispers will quiet. The loveseat will accept its place.

199

When teaching, I heard the student complaint "I am bored" more than once. I had a ready lecture: "Boredom is a state of mind. Something you impose on yourself. No one can make you bored. You are choosing to be bored."

And if I were in a mood, I continued, "Politician John McCain was a prisoner of war in Vietnam for over five years. For two years of his captivity, he was placed alone in a windowless, hot room. Solitary confinement. Did he complain of boredom? No. He kept his mind occupied, thinking about history, maps, the meaning of life; he wrote plays and novels in his head. He survived—physically and mentally— because he chose not to be bored."

In Florida, Jim, Teddy, and I had to sometimes figure out how to combat evening boredom. Teddy decided to hide in his room. Happy. Jim and I watched television together. I was able to binge watch 2.5 episodes of *Ozark* with Jim. The show, however, was too dark and stressful for me.

My attention drifted. I found myself stealthily looking at the Crockett Doodles website on my phone. Jim sat mere feet from me while I secretly enjoyed the fantasy of dog ownership. I almost filled out the puppy application twice. There was no obligation for just filling out the application. I dreamed of a Goldendoodle with an apricot coat and a little splash of white on her chest. Named Adele.

Abandoning my dog dreams, I asked Jim to watch *Top Chef* or *The Voice* instead of *Ozark*. Competitors get voted off the show, but no one is dissolved in acid, thrown off a high-rise balcony, or stabbed in the neck with a needle full of poison.

200

I let my gas tank get low. A habit. A routine. The dash screen told me I had only 10 miles of gas remaining. Then. Empty.

At this point, I had my reoccurring thought: I have been told by more than one person that the gas-to-mileage display on the dashboard is a lie. Intentionally inaccurate. Adjusted to compensate for humanness. Supposition: Some humans will push it to zero or beyond before actually stopping to fill up. If this is true, a zero reading is not really zero. At zero miles of gas left, additional miles remain. Some indeterminate number. I do not know if this is true.

While I frequently push my car to just 10 miles of gas remaining, I instantly get panicky at the 10-mile mark. At 11 miles remaining, my brain is calm. No inner dialogue. At 10 miles, my mental self-talk kicks in: "Oh my gosh, get fuel NOW!" Ten is my rock bottom.

I have it in my head that it would not be thrilling in the least to push
past 10 miles remaining to 9 miles remaining. Then, 8. Then, 7. Then, 6.
Then, 5. Getting quite nervous. Then, 4. Then, 3. Hyperventilating. Then,
2. Then, 1. Then, zero. At zero, if my car kept running, how would I feel?
Grateful? Indignant? Cheated? Angry? All of the above? If zero isn't
zero, what is it? A line to be crossed? An empty threat? An obstruction of
free will? Nihilism? Enlightenment?

I filled up with gas at 10 miles remaining, maintaining world order. My
dashboard now read 568 miles remaining. I sighed a mental sigh of
relief. Predictable. My inner Huck Finn—squashed.

201

As Teddy entered his twelfth-grade year, I began looking for a new Head
of Middle School position. We wanted to feel cold. We wanted to be
closer to family. Airfare and car rental costs had exploded since we first
moved to Florida, making visits to family unaffordable.

A recruiter sent my paperwork to a school in New York. Located just five
hours from each daughter—except for Marne who was in North Carolina.
The New York location was interesting. I was invited for a visit. The visit
went well. I received a generous job offer. I accepted.

202

Bits and pieces of my Introduction to Psychology class still play
around in my head, especially the term object permanence. I love the
weight of it. Object permanence. It sounds like something trustworthy.
Psychologically speaking, object permanence describes the ability to
know that objects continue to exist when they cannot be seen or heard.

As Jim and I packed up our house for the move to New York, I knowingly and incorrectly used the term object permanence to describe any object we decided to pack and move. Some of our objects were left behind—never to be seen or heard from again. No object permanence. Our piano, for example, was picked up—loaded into the back of a Tesla and driven away. I didn't believe it would fit. It did.

Jim was rather doggedly in favor of object impermanence. And I mostly agreed with him. A fresh start without clutter. That said, I kept the metal turkey that sat on top of our former piano. I bought the turkey at a Meijer grocery store for a dollar—back before Jim and I married. The metal turkey was discounted because it was damaged goods: the red paint on the turkey's snood (the red thing that hangs over the beak) was scraped down to the dull grey metal. I was newly divorced and broke. I took the wounded turkey home and fixed its snood with some red nail polish. That same week, my daughters and I had hot dogs on Thanksgiving. An affordable meal. But we also had a turkey. The metal turkey.

The rusty horseshoe that hung above the secondary entrance to every home Jim and I have shared also went with us. Three homes and counting. Our hypocritical good luck charm. We packed our speckled brown Texas Ware mixing bowl. Light and utilitarian. A prized possession. About five years ago, when Jim was out of town, I purchased a miniature cast iron statue of a Rottweiler dog at Golden Gate Nursery. I never named the dog; still, I felt oddly compelled to take him with us. He is rather stoic. And he is only small heavy. Not big heavy.

When moving, the weight of an object is inversely proportional to the likelihood of establishing permanence in our lives. My exercise equipment—a treadmill, elliptical, and stationary bike—had no chance. Purchased in Florida. Stayed in Florida. Too heavy. No tears.

203

We had an agreement. Jim would get all things outdoors ready for putting
our home on the market; I would get all things inside the house ready.
A straightforward arrangement. But Jim went to the Miami Boat Show.
I had three days unsupervised. I thought, "I'll get the back patio power
washed while Jim is gone." Rationalization: A gift to Jim. Reality:
Cleaning ceiling fans is underwhelming. Mind-numbing. Power washing
is transformational.

I met the power washer in the morning and then headed off to work. A
little later in the morning, I get a text from him: "Hey there, give me a
call when you can. Please." I called back. He told me there is no water—
it stopped. He packed up and agreed to return. I made a quick run home
in the middle of the school day. Yep, no water. I called Florida Soft Water
who showed up with impressive speed and fixed a blown fuse in the
watershed. All good, right? No. The power washer could come back to
finish the job until Saturday. Jim was expected home on Friday.

You know what looks worse than a dingy patio? A half-cleaned patio.
Not so transformational.

Jim texted that evening, "Back at the motel. I love you."

I texted back, "I love you. Remember that."

Jim replied, "That seems ominous."

I didn't say anything about the patio. I let Jim enjoy his adventure.
This was not about the patio anyway. I was looking for a quick fix. I
wanted seven years of grime gone in seconds. Wiping baseboards wasn't
cutting it. I have never tried a cigarette. I have never tasted beer. But I
caved to the allure of the power washer. I am sure it is a gateway drug of
some sort.

204

In the weeks immediately prior to Teddy's high school graduation, I frequently caught myself looking at Teddy and thinking, "Is he ready?"

When I did this, he said, "Stop looking at me."

One evening, Teddy came out of his bedroom sanctuary with a big smile on his face. Obviously, something had happened. Jim said, "What?"

Teddy replied, "Give me a minute." He walked to the kitchen to get a glass of water. Teddy then shared his computer screen with us. Teddy was accepted to one of his top choice colleges. Jim and I smiled with Teddy. Two or three seconds of complete, quiet happiness.

I broke the silence. "Well, there are other schools and more forms to fill out." And I proceeded to list all the college application work that remained for Teddy.

Jim said, "Can we enjoy this moment a little longer?"

Teddy replied, "Dad, Mom is just being herself. We need to let her be that." I decided to accept Teddy's words as compliment.

205

Jim and I sold our camper. More moving prep. I did not drop the camper blankets off at Goodwill. The quilts were in good condition.

Tommy Bahama quilts. A map-like pattern, cream background with brown-hued land masses: Bahamas, Florida, Jamaica, Cuba, Haiti, Dominican Republic. With compasses, palm trees, and sailboats scattered here and there. Superior in softness because they are broken in—perfectly. Memories of camping trips. I put them in a tub to move with us.

I still had our original set of camper quilts stashed in a bedroom closet from when we last moved from Michigan to Florida. Martha Stewart brand. Purchased on clearance. Brown and red, horizontal stripes with touches of floral accents. Still beautiful, despite a few worn spots and one noticeable stain. I packed them, too.

I packed the retired quilt from our Michigan bedroom—a brownish paisley, floral pattern. A 50% off at Kohl's purchase. This quilt has holes and is worn to its last layer of fabric. It still lives a good life though. I get it out in the middle of the night when the air conditioning shifts from just keeping up to freezing cold. About 1:00 a.m.

We no longer have twin beds, but I packed the two blue plaid twin-sized duvet covers. Pottery Barn. Hand-me-downs from my sister Jennifer. From when the girls lived at home. Twin beds were numerous. Double sets of bunk beds. I packed a second set of twin quilts. An antique blue floral pattern on a crisp white background. Maybe someday. Twin beds again.

I packed a stack of quilted pillow shams in with the quilts. I love pillow shams. Jim feels differently. He is a vocal pillowcase loyalist. He says shams are aptly named. Shams.

206

At the very top of the guestroom closet sat the Aquaman figurine still in its box. Never opened. A birthday gift for Teddy who unwrapped the present and said, "Why did you get me this?"

Teddy had forgotten that we saw the movie Aquaman together at the Silverspot Theater just a couple days after he broke his arm. The Silverspot is now closed, soon to be replaced by Alamo Drafthouse Cinema, which means our Aquaman movie memory has achieved collector's item status. Impossible to replicate. Sometimes, though, the value of a memory goes unrecognized for years. And years. No worries. The Aquaman figurine can wait. Unboxed. He is patient. I packed him.

207

Sophie Face-timed me to have my granddaughters Mary and Stella thank me for sending them two Live Wildly sun protection swim shirts.

Was it wonderful to receive a video call from Mary and Stella? Yes and no. They wanted to do more than talk to me. They also wanted to show me how they had mastered the front flip on their backyard trampoline. I have a fear of trampolines. I cannot watch. I abruptly ended the Facetime call as Mary and Stella, full of unbridled, courageous joy, ran towards their backyard trampoline. They had no stress. I did.

Jim and I felt stress when selling our house. I even Googled "how to manage the stress of house selling." I stumbled across a study that ranked the 10 most stressed states in America: 1. Tennessee, 2. Alabama, 3. Oklahoma, 4. Louisiana, 5. Nevada, 6. South Carolina, 7. Georgia, 8. Arizona, 9. West Virginia, 10. Indiana. The amount of stress attributed to each state was based on the statistically determined level of four types of stress: money stress, work stress, health stress, family stress.

I found the study metrics overly complex. Only two questions need to be asked: How many trampolines are in the state? How many residents are in the process of selling a home? Rank accordingly.

208

We sold and closed on our house—even though the realtor said, "This contract has hair on it." Jim and I loved that expression. It closed anyway. Hair and all. Our realtor was a genius.

We moved. After a couple of months working in New York, I realized my new school was not a fit. An unexpected surprise. Out of left field. Jim was on a fishing trip with his brothers. I texted him that I quit my job. All our belongings were in a New York Pod warehouse. We had made an offer on a New York house. Deposit lost.

I called Jennifer, "I quit my job. May Jim and I temporarily move in with you?"

"Yes."

Jim and I drove separate vehicles from New York to Michigan. The alone time was probably necessary to process the upheaval on an individual level before tackling it as a couple. The move to New York was a significant net loss. Financially and professionally.

209

We now lived in Ann Arbor with Jennifer and Scott. And their dog Milo. A Cavalier King Charles Spaniel.

I hadn't been to a University of Michigan football game since September 14, 2013. The Akron Zips played the Wolverines at the Big House. Pre-Harbaugh. A surprisingly close game, but the Wolverines won 28-24.

210

When I was growing up, if I were to have looked in the mirror and questioned, "Mirror, Mirror on the wall, who is the fairest of them all?" the Mirror would have responded, "Jennifer." Jennifer is a bit intimidating. A federal judge. Plus, she has journaled her daily exercise, type and time, since high school.

I was no slouch to exercise when I was younger but in more of a start-stop-start-stop-start-stop pattern, varying lengths of commitment and noncommitment. I occasionally mess with Jennifer's paradigm of order. A privilege of my birth order. Youngest sister. The baby. Jennifer typically ignores my juvenile jabs.

Once, however, as we were exercising together. I said to Jennifer, "You know, since I have not exercised as regularly as you over my lifetime, I have not worn down my joints and such. So, of the two of us, I am in actually in better shape to tackle exercise as we age."

Jennifer looked at me with annoyance, but I detected a momentary hesitation, a need to consider and dismiss the myth of my logic. Well concealed, but I could tell. Her brow furrowed in a very judge-like way. It took her about ten seconds to deem my nonsensical argument nonsense. I consider that a win.

All sibling baggage aside, I love Jennifer world.

211

I also love the Downtown Home & Garden Store in Ann Arbor, Michigan. It has an eclectic mix of well-known labels: Stormy Kromer Hats, Le Creuset cookware, Keen Utility work boots, Smart Wool socks, and Carhartt clothing and more Carhartt clothing. After browsing around the store, Jim bought me a beautiful blue Polish Pottery platter—the glazed surface is sprinkled with beautiful lapis-colored flowers, and a delicate blue dragonfly is located a little off-center. I love it, especially the dragonfly.

The store also sells what might be considered inferior merchandise. Trinkets without a recognizable brand name. A while back, I purchased a fist-sized ceramic figurine called the "Bluebird of Happiness." Price tag, $3.99. The two stickers on the bottom of the bird read "Frost Resistant" and "Made in Vietnam." The note of frost resistance suggests the statue might be placed out-of-doors; however, my Bluebird of Happiness sat on the ledge of a windowsill above our kitchen sink. When I had a kitchen sink. I was currently houseless. I love the bluebird. Ceramic love, not true love.

I know the bluebird won't bring me or others happiness, but I still sometimes like to think magic exists. I picked up an extra Bluebird of Happiness and gave it to my eldest daughter Sarah. Do not tell my other four daughters. While they might actually be relieved not to be burdened with the cheap figurine, they might also question-demand, "Where is my Bluebird of Happiness?"

My defense: If I had originally bought five Bluebirds of Happiness and given one to each daughter, they would have dubbed it the act of a crazy person. Then, en masse, they would rename the bird something jokingly clever. The Bluebird of Mom's Delusion.

212

Sometimes I turn into a human Magic 8-Ball, relying on rote responses when life feels hectic. I find myself saying, "As I see it, yes." "Don't count on it." "It is certain." "Ask again later." If my sister asks me to go walking or go to dinner, I respond, "Cannot predict now." Jennifer is no slouch and is onto my game and verbally counters, "Shake it and look again." I am not kind to my daughters when I am in 8-Ball mode. When they call to ask if I can talk, I respond, "My reply is no."

213

I found a new job. Teaching. In Ann Arbor. I love the school. The people. The work.

Jim and I bought our fourth house. Surprise—more a shack than a ranch, built in 1876. A former tavern, if local lore is accurate. A little house on a big corner lot. Black Walnut and Hickory Nut trees. Small houses have served us well.

Three daughters live close. Two daughters currently live out of state. Pennsylvania and Oregon. Jane lives a hop, skip, and a jump away in Chicago. Chris, in Florida. Jennifer, just a few miles down the road. Teddy goes to college less than two hours away.

Jennifer quickly absorbed me into her fitness routine, inviting me for 4-mile walks. Often. I joined Planet Fitness. She joined as well. I ask-demanded that Jennifer sign up for the Dexter-Ann Arbor Run with me. We did not run. We walked the 10K. At the last minute, Corrine signed up to run the 10K. It felt like a real family event now— cross generational.

Jennifer and I tackled the 6.2 miles at a 16:47-pace. I finished 16th out of 17 racers in my age bracket. I did better overall: 905th out of 941 10K participants. My underwhelming statistics did not dampen the experience. I was there. I finished. Jennifer and I were both way too giddy when we received participant medals at the finish line. We had not expected to get a medal. I know there are divisive politics regarding participation medals but getting that medal felt wonderful.

Corrine ran at an 8:13 pace, finishing 3rd out of 71 in her age bracket. She won a plaque and received a participation medal. She was beaming. Sharing her happiness was better than receiving a medal. But I do love my medal.

214

Jim was fishing with his brothers on Mother's Day—not that it matters. He is not my mother. He reminds me of this every Mother's Day.

I made plans to lunch with Teddy who was completing his first year at college. I drove up to his college and we headed over to Latitude 42, a restaurant Jim discovered when we lunched with Teddy on Easter.

The day was beautiful;the restaurant, full. Teddy and I were seated on the back patio. A nice table. Private. I ordered a Great Lakes Dip sandwich. I have a thing for dips. Teddy opted for next-level Mac & Cheese, cavatappi pasta, chicken, cheddar and gouda cheese. As we waited for our food, I began with my standard questions.

"Are you keeping up with your laundry?"

"Yes, Mom."

"Are you doing your homework?"

"Yes, Mom."

"Did you take care of next year's housing?"

"Yes, Mom."

After my interrogation, we laughed and talked about a range of topics—the waiter, summer plans, his sisters, our recent trip to Oregon. And when our food arrived, we talked about the food. Very pleasant.

As the meal was winding down, Teddy decided to shift the conversation to a Mother's Day topic. I expected praise.

"Mom."

"Yes."

"I think you should have touched me more when I was growing up."

"Teddy, really, do you know what day it is? Mother's Day. Compliments, please."

"I know. I love you. I just think you should have touched me more."

"We have a close relationship."

"I know."

"Teddy, I tucked you in every night. I kissed you good night on your forehead every night. Still do when you are home. I played with you, walked with you, talked to you, made sure you had food to eat, washed your clothes, helped you through tough times, laughed with you, cried with you, paid your college tuition. You had clean underwear."

"I know. No judgement."

"Listen. I spent the first two months of my life in an incubator. Rarely touched by human hands. I am doing my best."

Teddy smiled. He has heard this story before.

215

My husband and his sister Kay see each other sporadically. Every few years. She lives in Arizona. Kay once arranged to meet her brothers in the Keys for Winter Break. Years ago.

When Kay showed up, she cried tears of happiness. We had a wonderful visit with Kay. She is intelligent and funny. Distinctly Kay. Throughout the days of shared family time, Kay shed frequent tears, anticipating separation before it happened. We teased Kay in the way families tease each other, relentless and loving. Kay is hardwired to feel time, each moment, as it passes. Its beauty and confounding brevity.

I tend to be dense about time. Over and done before I even thought to remember it would be gone.

Acknowledgments

Thank you to Max F. Dama, Steve Dama, Sophia Fay, Jennifer Gorland, Axel Kallesøe, Marlene Miller, Brandi O'Neill, Emery Pence, Corrine Potocki, Melisa Potocki, Jane Reid, Nicole Ramos, Jimmi Stevens, and Heather for the encouragement and financial support. Much appreciated.

Thank you to Sarah, Sophia, Olivia, Marne, Corrine, and Tadeusz for surviving my imperfect parenting and giving me so much in return. And Eric, Devon, Nathan, and Taylor for loving the people I love.

Thank you to Grayson, Jillian, Jack, Mary, Stella, and Oscar for inspiring me with your intelligence, creativity, and energy.

Thank you to James Potocki for being born, being you—and everything else. So much else.